BONE SAW

PATRICK LACEY

PMMP

Perpetual Motion Machine Publishing
Cibolo, Texas

www.PerpetualPublishing.com

Cover art by Lori Michelle

ALSO BY PATRICK LACEY

Dream Woods

We Came Back

A Debt to be Paid

Sleep Paralysis

PRAISE FOR BONE SAW

"[*Bone Saw*] is a pulpy work of 1980s-styled, B-grade, gorehound fun. The story of Pigfoot, in both his cinematic and present-day Bass Falls murdering machine incarnation, is entertaining and properly gory."

—Michael Patrick Hicks, author of *Broken Shells*

"If you have a weak stomach, then you probably shouldn't eat before reading. [...] This is one of Patrick Lacey's best. If you love slasher films, then you will love this book."

—Cedar Hollow Horror Reviews

"It's almost like a slasher movie version of *Night Film*. [...] Lacey knows how to jack up the suspense and ladle out the gore. Once I started reading, I read it in two sittings. The ending was the bloody hell I knew it would be."

—Dangerous Dan's Book Blog

For Emily, my beautiful plot twist.

R OBERT JENKINS PULLED the sheet over his head but the brightness persisted, like the sun was flipping him off.

Fuck you too, he thought. He'd been trying to sleep for several hours but his migraine to end all migraines could no longer be ignored. There was a bottle of aspirin and week-old water on the bedside table. He popped three pills into his mouth and downed them. He stood and stretched, nearly falling twice as he made his way to the bathroom and took a never-ending piss.

Earlier that night, he'd had a few too many beers with the boys—a few being closer to a dozen. It was obvious he had a problem but at least he had a good reason. Beth was dropping off Lisa for the weekend, which was enough to put him over the edge. He saw his daughter twice a month, as stated by the divorce agreement, and each time she seemed to hate him more and more. The guilt was enough to drive him to drink and drink he had. And now he couldn't even sleep off his hangover-in-progress.

He belched up something sour and took a deep breath. The room was just starting to slow its spinning when he heard noises. Voices shouting. Machinery of sort running outside. Were they doing construction on a Sunday morning? How the hell early was it?

He left the bathroom without flushing and nearly fell again when he looked at the clock. It was two in the morning. He'd gotten home and collapsed into bed around midnight, waiting for sleep to arrive. The thing had to be broken. He'd used it for years, had gotten it as a wedding gift. It was malfunctioning just like his marriage had, only the clock had lasted longer. How about that? He made to turn it off when he saw movement through the window and was reminded of the sounds.

He brushed the curtain aside and almost shit his pants.

More than a dozen people stood in his backyard, all of them running around and spitting orders at each other. The source of the light was not the sun but two professional grade spotlights, shining on his home. He held a hand out to dampen their glow. A man sat in what looked like a director's chair while another guy with a clipboard asked him questions. The director nodded, sipping at something in a paper cup and rubbing eyes that looked just as hungover as Robert's.

It was a movie crew. There was no denying that. A sound guy held a boom microphone and two cameramen changed lenses. A special effects guy peered into a tub of dark red goo. Bits of latex body parts floated around. A pearly white bone that could have been a femur briefly surfaced to the top before sinking again.

A nightmare. Robert was having a nightmare. He often got them from stress and booze and when you put the two together, you had this fucked up fantasy. All he had to do was pinch himself hard enough and he'd wake up in the real world. He'd still be alone and drunk and he'd still be seeing his disappointed daughter today but at least he'd be sane. Whatever secret message this dream held, he did not wish to know its meaning.

The crew looked up toward his window and pointed at him, like they were getting ready to make a move.

Make a move? What the hell did that mean?

He shivered and did not answer the question for himself.

Outside the director stood from his chair and kept his eyes glued on Robert. The man nodded once and Robert waved, feeling immediately foolish.

Pinch yourself and make it quick. This thing's about to take a seriously messed up turn and you're going to piss yourself in your sleep. Grown men do not wet the bed.

He grabbed a patch of skin on his sweaty forearm and pulled the flesh taut, applying pressure. It didn't seem to do anything. In fact he could feel the pain like this was reality. He dug harder into his skin until his thumbnail went too far. A small crescent-shaped wound appeared, beading blood that looked similar to the special effects in the vat outside.

He did not wake up. The crew remained and the director still watched him.

Robert backed away from the window just as the director raised a megaphone and spoke into it. He said only one word but it was enough to make Robert scream like an infant.

"Action!"

The crew began rushing around. The two cameramen stepped onto his front porch and wood splintered. Eventually he heard the door bust open and the sounds grew closer.

He ran to the phone and dialed 911, thinking how crazy he would sound, but there was no dial tone. He tossed it against the wall and the screen shattered.

He looked out the window again. The director was still watching. Something darted from the corner of Robert's yard. It looked like a person in one of the most convincing monster costumes he'd ever seen. Its skin was an odd shade of pink, with mud and dirt caked onto arms and legs that looked only partially human. It rushed toward the house.

The footsteps downstairs multiplied as they entered the living room and kitchen then climbed the stairs. Robert ran toward the bureau and shoved it in front of the bedroom door. He backed away as the sounds grew closer, telling himself he'd lost touch with reality and he was glad Lisa was not here to see him like this.

Something banged on the door. It was not a polite knock. It was not asking to be let in. It was a demand and it shook the wood in its frame like an earthquake.

The window. The drop would quite possibly break his ankle or leg but it was better than whatever had just entered his home. Shouts and orders echoed through the wood. Someone asked the effects guy for more blood. The cameramen told everyone to get the hell out of the shot. Then the director's voice rose above the others.

"Break it down and let's get this over with. Make him scream and make sure you get in close on his face when he shits the bed."

Something grunted in response. It was the least human thing Robert had ever heard and he began to cry, something he hadn't done since his first week of sleeping alone. He backed away from the door and opened the screen when the grunting thing from outside smashed through the wood.

The blinding light was back and he couldn't see much aside from moving shapes and cameras and a seven-foot-tall creature that snorted as it grabbed his legs and pulled him to the floor. He tried to fight the thing's grip but its hands were the size of bowling balls. It sniffed at his neck and face. Warm slobber splattered against his skin. He tried to breathe but the weight of the thing was crushing his mid-section to the point of suffocation.

The picture of Lisa on his bedside table was turned around. He always faced it away from him when he went to bed. Otherwise her disappointed eyes bore into him and sleep became impossible. Now he wished the picture would magically spin around. That way he wouldn't feel so scared to die.

The thing on top of him thrashed and clawed at Robert's face. The pain was immediate and did not let up. Blood flowed like a river, soaking the carpet beneath him.

The director stood behind the creature and nodded to Robert. Perhaps he would have a change of heart and call the whole thing off. "Let's finish up. I'm hungry."

The grunting thing let out one last squeal before leaning over and taking a bite out of Robert's face. Most of his nose and lips came away in one pull.

The world turned a dark shade of red and his head flopped toward the picture frame. Lisa still faced away but he knew the image by heart. It had been taken during a tropical cruise a few years back. She was smiling and the sun was shining and that was good enough for him.

The thing came in for another bite and the director yelled, "Cut!"

THEY CALLED IT the Pigfoot on account of the snout and pink skin, not to mention its hooves. It stood upright like a human, well over six feet tall, and had an enormous gut that jiggled as it chased the girl. Most of its body was covered in dirt and blood. It had been spotted all over New England, a local legend that turned out to be more than just a legend.

The girl had made the unfortunate decision to go camping just a few miles away from the Pigfoot's shack, *several* miles from the nearest road and even farther from civilization.

The beast had been feeding on a deer, crunching hide and bones without effort, when it heard her giggling. She was skinny dipping with her boyfriend, her perfect body shimmering in the sunlight, and even though the temperature was nearly frigid and the lake was likely filled with leeches, she smiled after surfacing from a long dive. Her boyfriend, with his chiseled chin and chest, was nowhere to be found. Moments before he'd been preparing hot dogs over a fire and drinking his fifteenth beer of the day. She wiped water from her eyes, looked in every direction, and screamed when she saw the Pigfoot step from behind a tree. It held something in its clearly prosthetic hands. Something meaty and red with a face that slightly resembled said boyfriend save for the missing eyes.

She swam toward the edge and ran, not bothering to put on her bathing suit. Her breasts were impossibly large and round and surely fake. She screamed, her voice piercing and letting the Pigfoot know exactly where she was heading. At the most inopportune moment, she tripped over nothing in particular and rolled onto her back, rubbing her eyes and trying to fight through a daze. She screamed for someone, anyone, to please help her and she didn't want to die like this and she hated camping.

A branch snapped nearby. She wiped away tears that didn't seem to smudge her mascara and made to get up, falling back over when she saw the thing in front of her.

The Pigfoot stood no more than three feet away. She had to crane her neck to see its ugly face. It licked its lips and snorted, sending small drops of spit and her dead boyfriend onto her bare chest. She screamed again but it was cut off when the beast picked her up by the neck and tossed her like a twig toward the nearest tree. Her back collided with the wood and she nearly fainted. Her eyes were half open, just enough to see the Pigfoot walking toward her, kneeling down, forcing her mouth open, and biting off her tongue. The woman gurgled blood the color of hot sauce and watched as the Pigfoot began to eat the rest of her.

"Oh, shit!" Corey said, a cloud of smoke spilling out of his mouth and nostrils. He began to laugh, his snorting not unlike that of the Pigfoot, and it set off a chain reaction across the living room.

Marcus laughed so hard beer came fizzing out of his nose.

Jacquelyn, Corey's on-and-off girlfriend, howled, rolling on the floor and smacking the stained carpet like she was seizing.

The only one not giggling at the bright red blood and the latex mask was Liam Carpenter. He sat in his recliner, eyeing his friends and shaking his head. "Do we have to go through this every single time? You'd think they wouldn't be funny to you anymore."

"You'd think so," Marcus said, "but they always are." He wiped drops of beer from his upper lip and tried to regain his composure.

"You have to admit they're not exactly Oscar material." Corey emptied the bowl and began packing it again. It was the fifth or sixth time since they'd started the movie.

"Fuck the Oscars," Liam said. "It's a club and nothing more. Who cares about them, anyway?"

Jacquelyn's laughter died quickly. She eyed Liam like he was threatening her boy toy. "Why don't you come off your high horse? You like this splatter shit. I get it. Naked chicks and guys—or pigs—with knives and all of that. It gets you hard and that's fine but don't act like you're better than us because you're the only one in the world who watches this stuff."

"Take it easy," Corey said, still not looking away from the weed.

9

"No, I won't take it easy. We go through this every time we watch one of these shitty things. Can we watch a real movie for once?"

Liam gritted his teeth and tried to look anywhere but her death stare. He imagined a knock at the door. She would get up, thinking it was the pizza guy, and she'd put on her best face just as the Pigfoot bashed through the door and devoured her in two quick chomps of his jaw. He shook his head and came back to the real world, disappointed that she was still talking.

"It's just low-budget garbage. They're nowhere near as good as most of the popular ones."

He drifted off again as she began to list every well-known horror movie ever created, as if that made them good. The paused image of Pigfoot glared at him, the girl's tanned leg hanging halfway from his mouth. He'd been watching this stuff since he was a kid, had started with the classics and worked his way up to slashers and giallo films and so forth. But once he'd exhausted those resources he longed for more. He'd decided to dig deeper and that's when he'd found the Pigfoot.

His walls were covered with horror posters, some of them from the "good" and "famous" ones but others were more obscure. His most prized of all his collection was the Bone Saw studios picture, signed by founder and director of the Pigfoot franchise, Mr. Clive Sherman. Liam had paid a hundred bucks for the thing on Ebay. It was probably fake but he didn't much care. To him it was as real as the rush he got from these low-budget masterpieces.

His eyes wandered from Clive and toward the picture of Heather Hollis. It wasn't a poster like the others. It rested on the coffee table, a small-framed photo, one of her first head shots after she'd moved to Los Angeles. She looked beautiful, her eyes a preternatural shade of green that still got his pulse racing. He hadn't seen those eyes since she'd left him the year before and he doubted he'd ever see them again.

An empty beer can collided with his head.

"Are you even listening to what I'm saying?" Jacquelyn's Boston accent quadrupled when she was angry, making her sound even worse than usual. And that was saying something.

"No, I'm not. And I plan to keep it that way."

She opened her mouth to continue but Corey finally took a break from smoking and stopped her. "Cut him some slack, will you? He likes what he likes and there's nothing wrong with that."

Liam silently thanked him and Corey nodded, the result of more than a decade of friendship. It was painfully obvious that Liam was still getting his shit together after Heather and dropping out of NYU and moving into his aunt's in-law apartment above the garage. It had been a hellish year to say the least but Corey had made it slightly more bearable.

Jacquelyn took the advice and dropped the subject. She grabbed Corey's bicep and sucked his face. He took hits from the bowl and breathed them into her mouth as she giggled. It was enough to make Liam gag.

Neither of them spoke for a while. Only the sounds of puffing and slurping lukewarm beer filled the room.

"What the hell do you want to do now?" Jacquelyn said.

Liam rolled his eyes. "I want to finish the movie if you don't mind."

She flipped him off, stood, and stretched. Her shorts were so low, the crack of her ass hung out. She didn't seem to care and neither did Corey. Marcus watched, his mouth hanging open like a panting dog. "Actually," she said, "I do mind. I'm tired and I've got class in the morning."

Liam looked from her to Corey. *Are you going to let her run the show like that?*

Corey shrugged, his eyes bloodshot and half shut. *The hell do you want from me? She's hot as hell and I'm too lazy to put up a fight.*

And with that Corey followed suit, standing up and putting away his baggie of weed. He high-fived Marcus and Liam, told them he'd see them around, and stepped into the hall. Just before the door closed, Jacquelyn stuck her head back inside and mouthed two quick words.

Fuck off.

After they left, Marcus downed another two beers and belched loud enough to wake the neighbors. He didn't say a single word. Instead he eyed Liam every so often and cleared his throat. They'd met through Corey and while Marcus was a good guy they didn't have a whole lot in common. They rarely hung out outside the group.

"What do you say we finish watching this thing?" Liam pointed to the television.

Marcus threw away the pile of empties. "I'll pass. I'm too buzzed for this kind of stuff. Later." He left without another word and Liam was alone in the cramped apartment above his aunt's garage. Clive and Heather eyed him from opposite directions. He could almost hear their thoughts.

Clive smiled. *Don't listen to them, kid. They wouldn't know a good movie if it bit them in their judgmental asses.*

Heather frowned. *You could've done something but instead you chose to be a loser. You're going to start drinking too much and hang yourself in the smallest, shittiest town in Massachusetts.*

Below them, still frozen in time, the Pigfoot watched as well, begging Liam to press play and watch the death scene for the hundredth time. For just a moment Liam thought Heather was right—had always been right. Maybe he *was* a loser and he ought to get his life back on track. Maybe he *should* go back to school and take notes from film professors who were failed filmmakers. Maybe he *could* get a better job than working at one of the word's last remaining video rental stores.

Maybe, he thought, *but not tonight.*

He pressed play. The screaming continued, the blood kept spilling, and the Pigfoot kept killing.

BRIGGS REACHED FOR the glove compartment, his car briefly drifting into the wrong lane. Had it been a bit earlier in the day he would've received blaring horns and a few middle fingers but it was almost midnight and he was the only one on the road. The closer he got to the shithole of a town known as Bass Falls, Massachusetts, the more he felt he was the only person still alive in the state. He hadn't seen a headlight for miles and the darkness of the trees and road was starting to give him the creeps.

His hand finally found the bottle of Robitussin. The top was sealed with crinkly plastic but he'd learned to open the protective layer with his teeth. Some brands had another foil seal under the cap, like the liquid would spill out if it wasn't properly protected, but he could remove it with his finger and thumb without looking away from the road.

Marvin Briggs Randolph was not one to condone

drug use. He hated pill poppers and meth heads and even stoners but he did not take cough medicine to feel high. It was something much more primal than that.

It's because you're so very sick, dear.

His dead mother's voice again. She'd been speaking more often these past few years. In his periphery, she sat in the passenger seat, an old and shriveled skeleton that smelled like moth balls and Pine-Sol. Even in death, she was a clean freak.

He finished opening the bottle and took a long sip. The suspension resembled blood and it tasted like coppery pancake syrup. It slid down his throat like a worm and made its descent into his stomach. Took the edge off immediately and his mother, much to her protest, began to fade away. Though it wouldn't be for long. She always came back.

He saw the exit for Bass Falls up ahead—if you could call it an exit. It was more like a black hole, the interstate highway ending at the sleepy tourist trap. It was as far as you could go, the edge of the world, surrounded by the Atlantic Ocean and approximately one billion tacky shops and boutiques. He hated places like this but his line of work often brought him to hell and back.

Briggs didn't have many friends but the few guys he played poker with never believed he was a private investigator. Hell, most people didn't realize the profession existed outside of movies. But it was a real job and it paid the bills quite generously. He always asked for half the money up front, half after the job was done, but his current client had given him a lump sum and promised to triple it if he followed through.

The job was simple: find one Maura Black and

bring her back home to Mommy, one Lisa Black. He'd dealt with runaways before. They could be tricky but there usually weren't any shakedowns involved.

Lisa had been different from his other clients. She wore jewelry that looked more expensive than his car, and her perfume smelled like the world's highest grade potpourri. Not exactly his normal clientele. "There's something wrong with my little girl," she'd said in his office, on the verge of tears. It was a line he'd heard hundreds of times.

He'd assured her these sorts of cases were almost always a misunderstanding. Maybe Maura had shacked up with a boy or had decided to rebel against her parents. It was an old song.

"No," she'd said. "It's not that. It's been three weeks. I'm no psychic but a mother knows her daughter better than anyone else and I can tell you something isn't right." She'd opened her mouth to say something more but closed it quickly. He wasn't sure what but he knew Mrs. Black was withholding information.

The road transitioned from woods to ocean front houses that probably belonged to celebrities. A half dozen restaurants claimed they had the best clam strips in the world. He yawned and found it hard to believe any teenager would choose someplace like this to run away to. Lisa had used the tracking feature on her daughter's phone and the last place it had beeped before it shut off for good was Bass Falls.

Tomorrow he would ask around town, holding up her picture to store owners, maybe some kids at the skate park—if Bass Falls even *had* a skate park. He'd need to keep a low profile. When cops got wind of a PI in their town they tended to get snippy.

He drove toward the shore and parked his car. On the beach were a handful of couples making out on blankets and watching the stars in between fondling. Briggs looked up to see what all the fuss was about. They looked like a bunch of white dots to him. Nothing all that special. For a moment the big dipper connected its dots into a different pattern, turning to an old frail woman's face. She opened her mouth, preparing to unleash a barrage of warnings about colds and flus and obscure diseases but he cut it off before it got its starry tongue moving.

He undid the cap of the cough medicine and took another sip. The big dipper became just a constellation once more. His pulse slowed some and he watched the ocean sway in and out, in and out. It was almost relaxing.

He drained the rest of the bottle, tossed it into the nearest trash bucket, and belched into the night. One of the love-struck couples stopped kissing and peered his way, disgusted.

He smiled and shrugged and got back in the car, wondering if the motels were as shitty as the town.

★★★

"What are you working on?" The waitress stopped cleaning the table and held up a hand. "Wait, let me guess. The script. You're working on the script."

Liam yawned and nodded. His eyes felt like glue and he was nursing quite the hangover. He hadn't gotten much sleep the night before and the moment morning had arrived, he'd gotten on his bike and ridden to Bass Falls Coffee House. On the table in front of him was a crumpled stack of papers, written in penmanship only he could read. It was only halfway completed, had had several false starts, and was positively awful. One moment he would consider it his best work and seconds later he'd loathe every piece of dialogue, every single scene.

"What's it about?" the girl said. "If you don't mind me asking."

He finally looked up from his work—if you could call it that. The girl ("Michelle" according to her nametag) was pretty this close up. He'd seen her around a few times the last couple of weeks but hadn't taken much notice. She had long dreadlocks and several piercings, beautiful in an unconventional way. Nothing like Heather. "It's a horror movie. Not a very good one but a horror movie just the same."

"Horror, huh? You mean blood and guts and naked chicks? That kind of thing?"

"Yeah," he said, giving her a death stare fit for Jacqueline. "That kind of thing."

She held up her hands, a bottle of cleaner in one and a dirty rag in the other. "Whoa. Down, boy. I wasn't judging. I've seen plenty of that in my lifetime. My mother took me to see them all the time when I was way too little. She didn't even cover my eyes. I was just trying to make conversation."

He sighed. She was being nice to him, wasn't judging him like just about everyone else in his life, and he'd snapped at her for no good reason. "I'm sorry. I didn't mean to be rude. I'm just used to having to defend my stuff, that's all."

"I get it. Trust me. So what's your horror movie about? Are we talking slashers or possession or what?"

He shook his head and nearly cracked a smile. "Not quite." He opened his mouth but stopped himself, realizing how it would sound out loud.

Well, you see, there was this really beautiful girl, right? And then there was this guy who loved movies—horror specifically. He wanted to be a director. She wanted to be an actress. Talk about a match made in heaven. But when they got to college everybody else realized how talented she was and started offering her bit parts in their projects. Then she left the boy and headed out west to become moderately famous. And the boy? Well, he started smoking too much weed instead of going to classes, wound up dropping out of school and moving back to his crappy hometown. Now he lives above his aunt's garage because his parents have disowned him. Oh, and he hates his life.

But that wasn't the true plot. Not exactly. In the screenplay the guy moved out west and became obsessed with the girl. He followed her everywhere, built a shrine to her in his shitty apartment, and filled it with body parts from all her admirers.

It wasn't exactly sane when you took into account this past year but it was helping him cope and he'd change it just enough to avoid any lawsuits. Not that he'd ever get the damn thing made in the first place. He looked up and saw Michelle still staring, waiting for his true response. "Let's just say there is a lot of blood and gore and maybe even a naked chick or two."

"Don't be a stereotype." She winked at him and asked if he wanted another cup of coffee. Refills, she reminded him, were free. He needed to be at work in an hour but he was late just about every day anyway. He nodded. She finished washing the table next to him and walked away.

He found himself staring at her ass, which was almost as good as Heather's. She spun around quickly at the counter and caught him in the act. She turned a wonderful shade of pink and rolled her eyes.

Liam took a long breath, tried to hide his embarrassment, and got back to his crumpled script.

He smiled as he wrote about decapitations and skinning flesh and a razor-wielding psycho. It was over the top, splatter not to be taken too seriously, a nice change from the tone he'd been working with up to that point.

The ideas came a bit quicker today.

✳✳✳

"You've got to be shitting me," Liam said an hour later.

His jaw hung open as he stared at the newly erected sign out front of Roger Street Video Rental, his current place of employment.

Going out of business sale.

He was still shocked they'd never changed the name after VHS died out. They'd only switched to Blu-rays in the last year and their selection was pitiful. He'd known the store's time was running short but he hadn't expected it to be *this* short. It was a small town, after all, and sometimes relics from the past stuck around a little too long. But today it looked like Roger Street Video Rental's time was up.

From outside he could see boxes stacked along the walls. The drama, comedy, and even horror display signs had been taken down. His boss, Scotty Allen, was unhinging a shelf near the back of the front room. He stubbed his thumb with a hammer and said fuck several times, though it was silent from outside the windows.

He opened the door and the normally ear-piercing jingle of the bells sounded even worse.

Scotty huffed and puffed and sucked at his thumb. For a moment Liam thought his boss would cry. "Hey there, Liam. How's it going?"

Liam examined the rubble that was just yesterday his full-time job, one that required little to no effort and actually paid pretty damned well. "Not so good, Scotty."

Scotty sighed, sucked his thumb for another few seconds. He looked like an overweight baby with an unkempt beard. "Yeah, I hear that. Look, I was going to call you this morning but figured I'd wait until you came in. And by the way, you're late." He laughed and Liam could hear sadness in the gesture.

"What the hell happened?" Liam picked up an empty DVD case. Its disc and cover insert had been removed. He wondered what movie had once been inside.

"It was sudden. I'll tell you that much. Not something I was expecting."

"I thought we were doing okay. I thought you said tourists were dumb enough to waste their money at a crap hole like this."

"I did say that and it was true. It *is* true. We could've probably lasted another couple years if we were stingy and played our cards right."

"Then why were we open yesterday and closing today?" Liam tossed the empty case onto the floor with the rest of the junk.

Scotty set the hammer down on the shelf and had several false starts before he finally got his massive body to stand up. His knees cracked loudly and he'd sweated through much of his shirt. "It's going to sound crazy but I'm telling you I'm not pulling your leg. You've been a good worker. Hell, you stuck it out longer than everyone else, didn't you?"

Liam nodded, thought of the rotating staff they'd had in the last year alone. No one seemed to last aside from him. He'd worked there part time all through high school and had graduated to forty hours once he dropped out of college.

"Damned right you did. That's why it pains me to tell you I took a wad of cash to shut this place down."

"Come again?"

Scotty nodded, wiped away yellow sweat from his face and neck. "Told you it sounded crazy. Last night we stayed open a bit later than usual. Not because I was trying to make some extra cash or anything but because I sat my ass at that front counter, put on a Spaghetti Western, and passed out for a good two hours. When I woke up there was a guy standing at the counter. He was older, looked kind of familiar but I couldn't place his face for the life of me. He was tapping his fingers on the counter like he was in a rush and I almost told him to fuck off before he even opened his mouth. Then we got to talking."

"Talking about what?"

"This is where it gets even crazier. The guy's apparently a movie exec, a director in fact."

Liam's ears perked at the word. "Director?"

"The whole thing seemed a little mafia-esque if you ask me. He told me he and his crew were making a movie in lovely Bass Falls and they needed a couple spots to keep their shit. He said the store was far enough away from the tourist stuff that he could have some peace and quiet. Said a place like this was on its last legs anyway. I was about to tell him I liked my job, that I wouldn't have kept it open for so long if I didn't. Then he took out his checkbook and wrote down a very generous number. I think I'm going to retire."

Liam's throat constricted. "So that's it? You're just going to take a pay day and close the store?"

"I know how it sounds, buddy. I can't say it was easy. But you know we've been struggling. Look, here's what I'm going to do. I'll give you a share of it, enough to keep you on your feet for a while. At least until you find something else. How's that sound?"

Before Liam could speak Scotty limped toward the counter, still catching his breath, and took out his checkbook, started scrawling. He didn't write for a long time. There's couldn't have been that many digits. He ripped the check away from the rest, folded it, and handed it to Liam.

"Oh, I meant to tell you," Scotty said. "Guy said he was doing a horror movie. Sounds like it'd be up your alley."

"A horror movie? In Bass Falls."

Scotty shrugged. "Unless he's lying. Maybe it's a porno. He did seem seedy."

Liam fought the urge to peek at the check, wondered if maybe he couldn't buy some movies at discount price.

"I think you might've known of the guy too," Scotty said. He'd found a Band-Aid and was covering his new wound.

"Oh yeah?" Liam said, barely listening. "Let me guess. Frank Henenlotter."

"Not quite. Clive something or other. Herman maybe?"

Liam looked up then and forgot all about his first and final Roger Street Video Rental bonus. "Do you mean Sherman? Clive *Sherman*?"

Scotty snapped his finger and winced as the Band-Aid came loose. "That's him."

Liam's mind spun through follow-up questions but he could only manage two words. "Holy shit."

IZZY CULLEN HAD the crowd by the balls. They were oohing and ahhing like she was a first-class act, not some hippy chick slumming it for the summer. Her tip jar had grown exponentially during the last few songs and if it kept up, she'd get herself a nice hotel room for the night, maybe grab a bottle of the cheapest wine she could find.

She ended the song, set down her acoustic guitar, and promised the crowd an encore in a few minutes. Tourists and families walked away quickly, the magic of her music over within seconds. She didn't mind. They'd already paid her and unless they were going to toss more into the jar, they could be on their way.

She counted her earnings for the day thus far. Sixty bucks and some change. She folded the bills, turning away from any onlookers. One would think it was safe around them. They were well off enough to come to Bass Falls, after all. But she'd been ripped off twice since she'd started playing here and she wasn't about to take any chances. Yuppies could be crooked too.

She tucked her guitar into its carrying case and pulled out a pint of cheap rum. It burned going down her throat but it took the edge off. And there was plenty of edge. She was doing okay out here but she hadn't thought it would be so stressful. Her lodging for the summer, when she wasn't having one-offs in hotels, was a twenty-year-old van inherited from her grandfather. It had died just as she entered Bass Falls, was tucked away in the woods a few miles from the shore. How was that for an omen? No one had bothered her yet but she still slept with a knife curled in her fingers. Sometimes she woke in the middle of the night and swore she heard things rustling leaves outside the weathered windows. Things and not people. That's what her mind always told her and it was nearly impossible to get back to sleep on such nights.

Izzy chose a different spot for her sets. She wasn't exactly sure her operation was considered legal. She didn't have a permit like you needed in the cities but out here, in this wasteland of fried seafood and bikinis, she doubted the police gave a shit. They were probably too busy staring at tits.

Fumes drifted from a nearby hot dog stand. She crossed the street and ordered two dogs with extra onions and relish. She devoured the first in less than a minute. Back home in Philly, the dogs tasted nowhere near as good. They did their steaks right but their wieners left something to be desired. She smirked, took a bite of the second dog, and nearly choked when she saw the man watching from across the way.

26

Smoke filtered out of his nostrils in thick streams, dragon-like. He did not smile or move. Izzy told herself he was spacing out or watching someone behind her. But when she turned she saw only the cook in the cart, frying peppers on the griddle and itching his sweaty lower back in the process.

The man snuffed his cigarette out in the sand and walked toward her. Her knife was in her pack but she always kept the pepper spray in the lower pocket of her cargo shorts. She tossed the half-eaten hot dog in the trash and began to reach for the spray but the man moved too quickly. He was coming to beat her, to rape her, to kill her, perhaps in that very order. Her fingers fumbled on the fabric.

She was too late. He stepped up to her, extended his hand, and she closed her eyes.

The warm weather had softened her. She'd let down her guard and now she was going to pay. When she didn't feel any pain, she opened her eyes again.

The man held out his hand for her to shake. He was familiar somehow, possibly a member of today's crowd, like he'd seen her play on more than one occasion. He smiled and a gold tooth twinkled in the sunlight.

"I heard your songs back there. Pretty damn good. There are a lot of performers around here and most of them sound like dying cats."

"Thanks. I guess."

His hand was still waiting for her. She shook it. His grip was a little too tight but he didn't seem all that threatening up close.

"Are you local?" He reached for another cigarette, offered her one. The possibility of it being laced crossed her mind, but it was probably just paranoia.

She accepted the offer and he lit the end for her. "Not quite. I'm just passing through." *That's one way to put it. More like you got in a fight with your parents and got sick of living in upper class suburbia. You had it made but you wanted to be a rebel and now you're here with this strange man.*

"Same here," the man said. "If you can believe it, I'm actually out here making a movie."

She paused, her eyes widening.

He nodded. "That's right. Not a Hollywood film by any means. Hell, the budget is probably less than what you pay for tuition."

"Still. That's pretty cool."

"Yes, it is cool. Problem is, a couple of our actresses dropped off at the last minute. You know how it is, they get out here in the summer. The water's warm and the guys are walking around like it's *Baywatch*. They get distracted, even more high maintenance than usual."

She nodded. "I've seen plenty of them around."

"Then you know it's hard to find good help. That's where you come in."

"Me?" She turned around again just in case he truly was talking to someone else. There was still only the hairy hot dog attendant.

"Yes, you. You play that guitar like a maniac. I'm not filming a musical but it takes guts to do what you do and I think we just might have a place for you. We can't pay much—if at all. But it'll get you some exposure and we can feed you. We'll put you up in a room for a few days."

"And what exactly would I be doing? Extra work or something?"

"The kind of thing we're shooting—it doesn't require extras. Not in the traditional sense."

"So you're saying I'd be up front?"

"Up close and personal with the camera. Dialogue and everything. How's that sound?"

She smiled and puffed. "It sounds . . . " *It sounds fucking crazy. Something is off here. This guy is hypnotizing. The longer you look in his eyes the more you already feel like a movie star. He's buttering you up for something and it's something bad.* No. She was being stupid. There was nothing illegal going on. It was a low-budget movie, probably some indie drama or something. It was an opportunity and she planned on taking it.

"Sounds like fun."

"It does, doesn't it?" Smoke poured from his nostrils again, obscuring the gold tooth for a moment before the cloud passed and the metal twinkled once more in the sun. He started walking away from the herd of tourists, waving her on, saying something she didn't quite hear over the waves.

"What was that?" She grabbed her stuff and tried to catch up.

"I said I hope you like horror movies."

BRIGGS LOOKED IN the mirror and saw two people. The first was his own reflection, the second was his dead mother. He studied the bags under his eyes, the eight o'clock shadow covering his jaw, and the ever-growing layer of neck fat that had gone beyond the point of no return. He should start exercising, eating better. Maybe lay off the booze and cigars. Not to mention the cough syrup.

It's too late for that, dear, his mother said. *You might as well face it. You're very sick and you need help. You need your mother's touch.*

When he looked away from the mirror, there was no one standing beside him, only thin air, smelling vaguely of sweat and mildew, but when he turned back, there she was.

Patty Randolph, who would have been almost ninety this month, stood next to him. Her flesh was pale and nearly translucent. Dark blue veins bulged through the skin, emphasizing the countless liver spots. Several bruises were visible along her shoulders. Seniors spotted easily. Especially dead ones.

Briggs shook his head, told her to shut up. He was fine. He'd gone for a checkup not more than six months ago. The doctors said his blood pressure was a bit high and he could stand to lose a few pounds but there were no imminent risks to his health.

Liars. Every one of them. Patty tisk tisked and placed her head on her son's shoulder. He shouldn't have been able to feel her touch, on account of her not actually being in the cheap hotel room with him, but there was a cool sensation, like chilled and ancient flesh tracing his skin. He shivered, closed his eyes, and wished her away.

You can't get rid of me. A mother has a special bond with her son, especially when he's an only child. That bond never quite breaks, not even in death. You look ill. Are you running a fever?

She touched his forehead with an invisible hand and for a moment it felt like her skin had finally fallen off. Only bones remained now and a hollowed out skeleton caressed him. He flinched, backed away and almost fell on his ass. She was still in the mirror, cocking her head and asking if he had a thermometer anywhere.

He told her to fuck off and reached for the bottle of cough medicine on the bedside table. It took a few sips but eventually she faded away, though she didn't seem far.

Cold sweat covered his body. He thought about showering but he didn't want to spend another moment in this cramped room with the smell of his dead mother floating about. He grabbed his shoes and hat and did not look in the mirror on his way out the door.

The sun cut into his eyes and temples like a scalpel as he headed for the main office. Last night, after nodding off at the wheel a half dozen times, he'd finally settled on a pirate-themed motel called Captain Roger's. A ceramic bust of a knock-off Black Beard stood in the front parking lot. His head had fallen off at some point, now held on with duct tape. A sign beneath promised the lowest prices in Bass Falls, which was apparently a swashbuckling deal.

The air inside the office was too cool after the summer heat. He itched Patty's nonexistent fingers away like head lice and the attendant behind the desk gave him a funny look.

"Everything okay?" She wore coke-bottle glasses and spoke with a vaguely southern accent. *What the hell are you doing up here?* he thought.

It pained him to smile but he did. "Everything's lovely. Do you mind if I ask you a question?"

She was writing something down. He leaned over and spotted a half-completed game of Sudoku. "Go ahead. There's an information kiosk out front. Got tons of maps and brochures and whatnot. The whole town's like a circle so it's pretty hard to get lost. I usually tell people to just pick a direction and stick with it."

He held up a hand to cut her off for fear that she'd keep talking forever. "I didn't mean about the town. I'm actually looking for someone." He dug the picture of Maura Black out of his pocket. The girl looked pretty enough, not unlike her mother, save for a few less wrinkles and what looked like much perkier tits. She was attractive but not a show-stopper, which meant she'd blend into a crowd. Bad news for him.

The attendant looked at the picture for a long time then raised her eyebrows. "You a cop or something?"

He itched at his stubble. "Or something. Have you seen her or not? She's not in any trouble and neither are you. Does that help at all?"

"No, it doesn't. And I'm sorry. I can't help you because I haven't seen her."

"Are you positive?" He thought about switching tactics and going for a bribe but the lady seemed more interested in her word puzzle.

"Positive." She looked back down, chewed on the eraser, and tried to work through the game-in-progress.

When she didn't look back up, Briggs returned to the heat. It was going to be a long day.

✱✱✱

He asked what must have been fifty people, most of them tourists as luck would have it, if they'd seen Maura Black. They all answered with a quick "no." The girl was smart. He'd give her that much. She'd covered her tracks like an expert, had emptied her bank account a few days before she left home and hadn't used her credit card once. He had access to certain software that wasn't entirely legal. It kept tabs on people, assuming they were on the grid, but Maura was keeping as low of a profile as she could. She did not want to be found.

Sweat soaked through his clothes. He hadn't brought any shorts and he regretted that decision immensely as he made his way toward the beach. There was plenty of eye candy and a dozen or more food vendors. If he could find some shade he could easily spend the better part of a day out here. His eyes were dry and red and if he closed them, he'd surely sleep for hours. But he couldn't quit just yet. There was work to be done and he wanted the rest of his pay.

Among the tourists and half-naked girls were several homeless men and women. They ate from trash barrels and mumbled to themselves. Each had their own rusty tip bucket in front of their spots and most of them were empty. Briggs scanned their faces, but the youngest looking woman had grey hair and deep, trench-like wrinkles. If Maura had taken to the street, she wasn't at the beach.

The girl had been away long enough that she might need some dough. If she was working it was under the table or else she would've shown up on his trusty software. Which meant she was at a smaller business or one of the hundred tourist shops in town, which didn't exactly narrow his search.

On his way toward the stone steps that marked the edge of the beach, someone grabbed him. For a moment he knew it was his mother. She was no longer an illusion or some fucked-up guilt trip. She was real and she'd risen from her grave and it was time for his medicine.

When he spun his head around he saw a mud-caked face with an equally mud-caked beard. The bum smiled. "Morning. Or afternoon. I'm not sure what time it is but you look like you'd appreciate a magic trick."

Briggs couldn't help but laugh. The man had a deck of cards laid out on the sand. He pointed to them and asked Briggs to pick one.

"Can't say I believe in magic. It's all a big con and I know how to con with the best of them. Tell you what. You answer a question for me and we can skip the trick."

"What kind of question?" The man folded up his cards and held onto them like they were his children. He'd been ripped off more than once.

The photo of Maura had started to crinkle at the edges. "You seen her around at all?"

The man studied the picture, squinting so that the whites of his eyes were lost within the dirty lids. "Pretty, ain't she?"

"Sure is."

"Can't say I've seen her. A lot of people come through here, you know? Most of them don't look our way." He held his hands out to the other bums, most of them sleeping face down on rolled-up shirts and towels. "Say, you're not with those movie people, are you?"

Briggs cocked his head. "Movie people?"

The man nodded. "That's right. Guy's been coming by every day, asking folks to star in his movie. I thought it was my turn yesterday but he asked my buddy Chet instead, promised him a shower and a hot meal. That's like hitting the lottery out here, you know? Only Chet ain't been back since. Way I see it, he's probably still working and making some money while he's at it. Good for him, that bastard."

Briggs rolled his eyes and returned the photo to his pocket. The guy was loony. No movie execs would dream of shooting out here. The scenery was nice enough but the city officials must have been hell to work with. Permits didn't come cheap in a place like this. He took out a five-dollar bill and slipped it into the can. "Thanks for your help. You have a nice day."

The man stood and called to Briggs as he walked

away. "You sure you don't want to see a magic trick? It'll blow your mind."

Briggs climbed the steps without answering.

✳✳✳

Just as Briggs was about to call it a day he saw her through the window of a shitty-looking coffee joint named, of all things, Bass Falls Coffee Shop. She stood behind the counter, taking some surfer-looking guy's order. Even from outside Briggs could see the guy staring at her tits. At *Maura's* tits.

He looked at the photo for the hundredth time and compared it to the real thing. She had dyed her hair from bleach blonde to dark brown. It was perhaps three inches shorter and had since turned to dreadlocks. She had three times as many piercings in her face and some kind of tattoo on her upper arm. Her mother would've done good to give him a newer photo.

He rubbed at his tired eyes and decided a cup of coffee was just what he needed. Maura was grinding beans and making a latte for the surfer when Briggs approached the counter. "Be right with you."

He smiled. "Take your time."

She finished up the order and came to the registers. This close there was no denying the resemblance. The nametag on her shirt read: *Michelle.* Bass Falls Coffee Shop certainly didn't look too deeply into their new hires.

"Michelle, can I just get a cup of coffee?"

She smiled, her lip ring jutting out just a bit. "Sure can. You want light, medium, or dark?"

"What do you recommend?"

"Depends on what you like, I guess. I'm a dark

roast person myself. I like it strong and bitter." She looked around and lowered her voice. "Just like my boss."

They shared a laugh and Briggs decided he would wait across the street until her shift was over. Then he'd follow her home, call the mother, and get the hell out of this shitty town. "Dark it is, then."

"Coming right up."

FTER THE DAY he'd had, a drink was in order. Liam had stuck around Roger Street Video Rental for another few hours to help Scotty pack things up. On the bright side, his boss gave him free range of the overstock in the backroom. There were a couple Bone Saw studio movies on VHS that he didn't have in his collection. He grabbed *The Pigfoot II* and *Cum Beasts from Mars* and tossed them into his backpack.

But movies or no movies, the money Scotty had promised would carry Liam until he found another job turned out to be one hundred dollars, about one-fourth his normal weekly paycheck. He almost ripped the thing in half as he stepped out of the store for the last time.

"Thanks again for all your hard work," Scotty had said, cracking open a can of Coors right there on the sidewalk. "Truth is, we would've probably closed a hell of a lot earlier if it hadn't been for you."

"Yeah," was all Liam could say before riding off. He wished he could've been more sentimental but he was too pissed off.

Flanagan's Pub was a half-mile away from Main Street and usually filled with locals, though there were a few tourists every now and then. They weren't hard to spot in the crowd of fishermen and hipsters.

Liam left his bike out front and headed inside. The smell of stale beer and cigarettes hit him instantly despite the "no smoking" sign posted over the door. He got a few looks from the clientele but most of them were harmless. He'd been coming to Flanagan's since the day he turned twenty-one and was just as much of a regular as the burnouts. Heather had told him the place was bad news. Only losers hung out there.

Liam grabbed a seat at the bar and ordered two PBRs.

"Someone else joining you?" Dave the bartender asked.

Liam looked at the front door and imagined, as foolish as it seemed, that Heather would enter at any moment. She'd given up her flashy life out west to come back to her shitty hometown with her loser high school sweetheart. They could finally get married and have kids just like they'd discussed on so many nights after fucking.

The door remained closed.

Liam removed his pack and set it on the floor. "Just me tonight, Dave. Trying to get a head start."

Dave laughed. "A man after my own heart." He poured two overflowing pints of the cheapest beer on tap and accepted Liam's money. Liam told him to keep the change.

"High roller tonight, I see."

"You don't even know." Liam examined his severance check for the tenth time, and tried not to grit his teeth.

He drank the first beer in four large gulps. It cooled his insides and went straight to his head so that things seemed just a bit less horrible than they truly were. He downed half of the second beer before deciding to take his time. He was on a fixed income now, after all.

He set the beer down on the counter and stared into the foam for a long time.

The guy to his right, a behemoth with a ZZ Top beard, stood, belched, and made his way out the door.

The man sitting two seats over slid to the open spot. "Nice shirt."

Liam winced. He didn't feel like talking to anyone right now. He wanted to get drunk, go home, get stoned, watch some horror movies, and pass out. Not unlike any other night when he thought about it. He remembered he was wearing his *Blonde Bimbo Massacre* t-shirt, one of the first Bone Saw films he'd seen. A classic tale of skanks wearing next to nothing who became infected by toxic hairspray before eating every person in sight. A masterpiece in other words.

Liam raised his head to see what kind of person, other than himself, would take note of the shirt. When he saw who was sitting next to him he thought for a moment he would either pass out or piss his pants or both.

It was Clive Sherman.

The alcohol coursed through Liam's veins quicker. He hadn't eaten since breakfast and the bar began to spin. "You're . . . "

Clive nodded and ordered a whiskey on the rocks.

"I haven't seen anyone wearing one of my shirts in years. We sell them on the website but they don't go as fast as they used to."

Liam nodded without blinking and finished his drink. To hell with money tonight. He was sitting next to his idol. Dave brought a third beer without being asked.

"You really are making a movie in Bass Falls." He wished he could retract the words. He'd sounded too childish, too star struck, even if it was the truth.

Clive smiled. His gold tooth glittered even in the dim lights of the bar. To Liam, the tooth had been the symbol of all things horror since he'd read an interview with Clive in the first issue of *Fangoria* he'd ever bought. Up close it was mystifying, like he was talking to a god.

"What's it about? If you don't mind me asking." He thought back to Michelle at the coffee shop. How he'd been annoyed at these same questions, how the tables had turned now.

Clive sipped his whiskey and looked somewhere past the bar. His eyes took on a dream-like sheen. "Does it matter? I used to tell myself I'd never make a film for a paycheck. I was making art, no matter how many people thought it was shit. But even I got sick of being on the bottom. I got a generous offer from an investor and I took them up on it. Now I'm stuck in this shitty bar in this shitty town making what I hope to be my last shitty movie." He set his glass down a little too hard on the counter. Dave eyed him for a moment then went back to making a drink.

"Does it have the Pigfoot? I read somewhere you were planning on making another sequel."

"Yeah, kid. It has the Pigfoot. And plenty of death and fucking too." He slurred his words.

Liam nodded, his eyes wide, feeling his buzz turn to something more advanced. A thought popped into his head but he tried to push it aside. *Don't say it. Don't make a fool out of yourself.* "You know, you're the reason I went to film school. I started watching your movies when I was a kid. They had a lasting effect on me. I thought if he can do it, maybe I can too."

Clive looked away from his trance. "That's great. I'm a role model. Let me ask you something. Did you even *finish* school?" He held up a hand as Liam was about to answer. "Because I'm betting you didn't. Especially not if you're hanging around here." He motioned to the regulars, most of them too drunk to notice the impending argument. "You think you're the first person to tell me that? I inspired an entire generation of morons. Everyone who's seen my movies thinks they can pick up a camera and do the same thing, only better. Don't take this the wrong way, kid, but fuck you."

Something snapped in Liam at that moment. The bar's temperature was too hot. His clothes felt itchy against his skin. He was tired and hungry and depressed and, as of this afternoon, unemployed. He was sitting next to his hero, the man who'd inspired Liam to pick up a camera and make something of himself, though he wasn't doing a fine job at that either. Everything from the last year came at him like a speeding bus and suddenly he hated Clive Sherman more than anyone in the world. "No," Liam said, "fuck you. You know that video rental store you bought for storage? That's my job—or was until a couple of hours ago. Is this how you treat all your fans? Your movies may be classics but you're an asshole."

Clive drove his fist into Liam's jaw. He fell off his stool and looked up, thinking, *What the hell just happened? Did Clive Sherman just punch me in the face?*

Blood seeped from his split lip and his jaw started to swell. He tried to get up but Clive kicked him down, held his foot onto Liam's chest. "Kid, you ought to watch what you're saying and who you're saying it to. Good luck with making your movies. Looks like you got blood on your shirt. Make sure you order another one." He pushed his foot down harder for a moment. Liam's ribs felt ready to crack. Eventually, Clive lifted his foot and left the bar.

Dave came around and helped Liam up. "Holy shit. You should go to the hospital."

Liam wiped his face and his hand came back red. "I'd rather just go home."

Dave walked him out the door. The night air felt good on his face. He could feel drops of blood cooling in the breeze as they dripped down his chin. "You got it from here?"

Liam gave him a thumbs-up and spat onto the sidewalk. He turned around to grab his bike but his hand touched thin air. It wasn't leaning against the wall where he'd left it. He'd never chained his bike once since he'd been coming to Flanagan's and tonight, out of all nights, someone had ripped him off. He would've sworn if it didn't hurt so badly to speak.

MARTY RANDALL'S EYES were caked with sleep and dirt and his mouth was drenched in drool. Before his wife Sally had died ten years prior, she used to make fun of the way he drooled in his sleep. He was an adult infant, she'd tell him, rubbing her swollen belly and asking how she was going to take care of two droolers in one house.

It was one of the last things he remembered before the gas line underneath their house caught fire and exploded, burning everything so badly the foundation smoked for just under a week. Marty had just stepped out to buy a pack of cigarettes at the variety store down the street. He heard the sirens as he lit the first one.

A decade later, Mart pulled from his pocket a pint of the cheapest whiskey he'd ever purchased and took two large gulps, hoping that the burning sensation and the oncoming buzz would help him forget his past, his present, and what little of a future lay ahead.

He'd pulled in nearly ten dollars today, thanks to the guy who'd been asking all those questions. He could grab himself some burgers at McDonald's and find a place to squat for the night. The shelter would be full by now. It must have been going on ten o'clock and they usually closed their doors around eight. He hadn't meant to drift off but the sun had been warm and the breeze had been lovely.

Now it was a bit too cool on his skin. He zipped his ripped sweatshirt and gathered his things, stuffed the dollars and coins into his pockets, and stood, wincing at the pins and needles in his feet. The tingling climbed toward his knees and he was paralyzed but not just from the lack of circulation.

Two men were digging a hole in the sand. They stood perhaps fifty feet to his left, smoking cigarettes and making what sounded like dirty jokes. There was a light propped above them, professional looking, almost like something . . .

Like something out of a movie.

They were with that director who had given Chet a part in the film. Marty blushed in the dark. He'd been chosen to have a role after all. He'd known something big was happening in town. When you didn't have a job or a house or a family you got to watching your surroundings. He'd seen the director sniffing around for weeks, perhaps location scouting. He'd watched the crew setting up miniature cameras all over town, not unlike the security cameras you saw at liquor stores.

Bass Falls had a summer blockbuster on its hands and Marty walked toward the men who were about to make his dreams come true. He lit a cigarette on his way. He'd quit for a while, couldn't stand to think that if he hadn't been smoking that day, he could've died with his family. But eventually he gave into the urges. They would kill him slowly and why should he be spared when his wife and daughter were in the ground?

A man carrying a camera and another with a tall microphone propped on a rod appeared from behind the public restrooms. This close Marty saw there was a tall rectangular object near the hole they were digging. It was covered with a black sheet. Every so often, the object shook and rattled. Marty licked his finger and tested the wind. It didn't seem all that strong tonight. Certainly not strong enough to shake something so big. His mind started working, internal warnings sounding, but he was too tired and too buzzed to take much notice.

One of the guys digging the hole pointed at Marty. Tattoos covered his arms and neck, the designs on his skin blending with the night. The other digger turned and got spooked, stepping back. His ears were pierced with large gauges, the lobes sagging like a member of some exotic tribe. "I thought he was going to be out cold when we do this?"

The other digger shrugged. "The hell do I know? It doesn't make much difference. Nothing about this shoot has gone according to plan, all things considered."

Digger number one nodded, his sagging ears flapping. "Yeah, you're right. Either way, the guy's here and that's good enough for me."

The cameraman stepped up to the hole and played with the lens. It was all so professional. Marty had wanted to be an actor when he was younger but it had seemed impossible. Now here he was. About to star in his first feature.

"Evening, boys." Marty tossed his cigarette in the sand and buried it with his shoes, the soles of which were threatening to tear off at any moment. "You're with that director fella?"

Digger number one nodded. "We sure are."

"I knew it. He said he didn't need me but I saw the way he stared, could practically hear the gears turning in his head. And here I am."

The cameraman finished fumbling with the machinery and whispered something to the sound guy, eyeing Marty nervously. The crew probably hadn't worked with homeless folks before. Marty was used to that look. He needed to gain their trust, to show them he hadn't lost *all* his sanity just yet.

The object beneath the sheet moved again and this time Marty was certain it wasn't from the wind. It sounded like something breathed beneath the fabric. "What's in there?"

Digger number two laughed. "Just some equipment."

"This is going to sound strange," the cameraman said, "but we need you to stand in this hole and let us bury you up to your neck."

Marty peered into the five-foot crevice and couldn't help but smile. "What the hell kind of movie are you guys making, anyway?"

The cameraman looked at the rectangle for a long time, his eyes wide. "Do you like monsters?"

Marty set his pack down and stepped into the hole. The bottom was moist and cool. He shivered. "Now you're talking. I used to watch Frankenstein and Dracula every weekend. Scared the shit of out me when I was a kid but I loved it too, you know?"

"We know," Digger number one said. On the side of his neck was a large panther tattoo, eyes glowing in the harsh light of the overhanging bulb.

They worked quickly to bury Marty up to his neck. He whistled and tried to remain professional. He wondered if they'd cut him a check tonight or if he'd need to wait until the film was released. Would there be royalties involved? He didn't want to ask. That would seem too desperate.

"What are my lines?" Marty said, thinking how he'd look in a real movie, if he'd seem convincing to whoever viewed the film. If only Sally could be here to see his debut.

The sound guy pulled the sheet off of the rectangle. Beneath the fabric was what appeared to be a cage and in the cage was something impossibly tall and pink and dirty and deformed. It had the face of a pig and the body of giant. It snorted and licked its lips, making eye contact with Marty's mostly buried head.

His internal warnings won out over the buzz and excitement. He struggled beneath the sand but the diggers had packed it too tightly.

The cameraman stepped toward him, studying his screen and trying to keep steady. "Don't worry about your lines. Just let our friend in the cage do all the work."

Metal scraped on metal as the sound guy undid a latch and then the door to the cage swung open.

Digger number one stepped back and nearly tripped. "No matter how many times we work with this thing, I'm never going to trust it. Who's to say it won't take a bite out of us and not the bum?"

"Clive said he's got the thing trained or something. Said he and Tara worked closely with it." Digger number two held the shovel up like a sword.

"We'll have to get a shot of it digging the hole after," the cameraman said.

"What is this?" Marty said, still struggling. It was no use. The sand was too damp. It had hardened like concrete and the circulation in his limbs was slowly fading.

The thing from the cage roared as it approached him. Pink slime dripped from its mouth, spit mixed with blood, plopping onto Marty's nose.

Marty screamed. Surely the thing wasn't real. It must have been a special effect, some animatronic beast that looked a thousand times more realistic than any CGI he'd ever seen. But this close he knew he was being naïve. There was no denying the thing's existence when it snorted and leaned toward Marty, eyeing him like a trough filled with feed.

"Wind's picking up," the sound guy said, lowering the microphone. "Let's hurry so we don't fuck up the shot."

The cameraman nodded, smiling, an overweight nerd who enjoyed burning armies of ants through his magnifying glass. "Get him, boy."

The pig thing sniffed Marty's face. Its breath smelled of shit and death and mounds of decaying garbage. It licked him and squealed.

Wake up, Marty thought. *You're still napping over there. This is just a fucked up nightmare. You're guilty about leaving that day, always will be, but it wasn't your fault. There are just some things that are out of your control.*

The pig thing grabbed Marty's head with two

hands the size of watermelons and squeezed. The pressure was enormous. He could feel his brain swelling, protesting against his skull, which began to crack slowly. His eyes were on fire, like they were being pushed from the inside out. He tried to scream but his jaw became unhinged. Several molars came loose and popped out of his gums. One of them dislodged into the back of his throat. He coughed it up and took a long breath of the salty air.

Then his breathing was cut off. As was his hearing and vision and taste and smell. The pressure grew to something beyond pain. His head imploded and parts meant for the inside flooded out, dripping onto the sand.

LIAM STOPPED TEN minutes into his walk home to catch his breath. Before high school he'd been on the track team and had run two miles each day. Then he'd gotten his first camera, began filming his own short films, and started fucking Heather. Those things took precedent over his health.

And look how far they got you.

Liam spat more blood onto the sidewalk. An egg-shaped bruise adorned his chin, swelling by the moment. He could feel his pulse through the throbbing, the pain like a tribal drum beat. Booze and pain blurred his vision.

His aunt's house was just five blocks north but the distance felt states away. Heather would've had a field day with this, reminding him he was pathetic. If he couldn't walk a mile without giving up, how the hell did he expect her to stay with him? He shouldn't have been surprised when she dumped his sorry ass.

He mentally told her to shut up and prepared to walk again when something moved in the bushes to his right. He stood in front of a Victorian home. It had once belonged to a poet or painter. He couldn't remember which. There was an informational plaque next to the front door but it was too far to make out the words. And he didn't feel like stepping into the yard on account of the bushes swaying violently like there was an approaching hurricane.

It must have been a raccoon or a stray dog, though the longer he watched branches of the bush nearly snap, the more he suspected it was much bigger. The thing made awful noises, something like growling and hissing and snorting all in one. Whatever it was, it did not sound friendly.

He backed away and jogged, not daring to look back. The sounds weren't drawing closer, he told himself. Those weren't footsteps just behind him, gaining by the second.

He picked up the pace, his lungs and injuries protesting. Head too heavy for the rest of his body. His good eye threatened to close. Just four blocks away now. He could make it.

Three blocks. The sounds were just behind him. Was that hot air on his neck?

He gritted his teeth against the pain and sprinted, gained some distance from his pursuer. He was going to make it. Fuck Heather and Clive Sherman and whatever the hell was chasing him. Fuck them all.

Something turned the corner ahead. There was no time to slow. He collided with the thing. It grabbed, raked its nails into him. Another feral animal like the one from behind. He was going to die in both directions.

The thing stopped flailing and he saw it was not a thing at all but a girl.

It was Michelle from the coffee shop. She was covered in sweat and her mascara was running. "Liam? From the shop? The script?" She couldn't speak more than a few words in between her panting.

He nodded. "We have to get out of here."

"Some creep is following me."

The thing behind Liam, now just one block away, snorted and shrieked.

"What the hell was that?" Michelle said, standing up and dusting off dirt from her jeans.

"I don't know and I'd like to never find out." He pulled her forward.

Two blocks away from his aunt's house.

Footsteps behind them. Gaining.

One block away.

Snorting and growling. Just inches away.

Liam turned the corner, pulled Michelle into his aunt's yard, and hid behind the shrubs. She opened her mouth to say something but he forced it shut with his hand.

His pursuer slowed to a stop just on the other side of the shrubs. It was too dark to make out many details through the branches but he could tell it was enormous, blocking out his view of the house across the street. It sniffed the air, sounded as though it licked its lips. It smelled rotten and for some strange reason, Liam had deja vu, like he'd been in this exact spot a thousand times before. That *thing* was—dare he say it—familiar somehow. He tried to push the notion aside but it stuck with him like a tumor.

Liam was certain they were dead as the thing peered through the bushes.

He closed his eyes and prepared for long claws to rip skin from bone, waited for jagged teeth to chomp through muscle like it was taffy. When the pain did not come he risked opening his eyes. Voices shouted from the direction he'd just run. The animal or rabid hobo or whatever the hell it was snorted once more before running off.

Michelle wiped sweat from her face, leaving behind black mascara streaks on her chin and cheeks. "I think you may have just saved my life."

He wanted to say something cool and heroic but only labored breaths came out. He pointed to the apartment above the garage. She helped him up and they walked toward the front door.

He swore he could still hear the thing grunting a few blocks over.

✳✳✳

What the hell did I get myself into?

Briggs lay beside a doghouse, across the street from the garage Maura and some kid with a messed up face had entered. He wondered if the kid was being played too or if he was in on the joke but there were more pressing issues.

Like the human-sized pig walking on two legs and screeching into the night. The thing turned toward Briggs and though he was hidden from its sight he could feel its pink fleshy eyes boring into him. It sniffed the air like it smelled a barbecue in progress. Just as it began to cross the street and close the distance he heard footsteps, approaching quickly from the right. He tensed and ducked down farther, thinking *now what? Is it cows this time?*

Eventually the pig thing screeched and retreated

in the direction it had been running. Moments later two men, one blanketed with tattoos and the other riddled with piercings, slowed to a stop. They leaned over and tried to catch their breath.

"I thought you said Clive had the thing trained?" Tattoos said.

"That's what he told me."

"And you believed him?"

"He's our fucking boss. And when your boss offers you that kind of money you don't ask questions."

Tattoos leaned against the mailbox, not more than five feet away from Briggs. If the guy turned around Briggs would be spotted and something told him he did *not* want to be spotted. These guys were working with the pig, whatever that meant, and the whole business seemed less than legal.

Less than possible.

"Look," the one with the piercings said. "Let's go find CJ. He's got the cage in the van and he's probably circling the neighborhood. We'll grab the Pigfoot, we'll head back, and we'll turn in for the night. Maybe check out some of the girls, huh?" He winked. "Clive brought in another one today. A hippy chick with a guitar. She still thinks she's going to be in a movie."

"Technically she is."

They shared a laugh and started jogging.

Briggs formed a checklist in his mind. In the last twenty-four hours he'd learned Maura Black was playing her mother and everyone else for some odd reason. Check. There was a guy walking around the beach and asking hobos and hippie chicks if they wanted to be in a movie. Check. And there was something called the Pigfoot marching around town, looking awfully hungry. Check.

What did all those things add up to?

He wasn't sure but it was something big.

For a moment he thought he'd finally drank too much of the red stuff. He'd studied the warning labels thousands of times. It caused jitters and loss of motor control and brain damage and, last but certainly not least, severe hallucinations. Maybe his mind had come unraveled and this was the beginning of the trip to end all trips.

Nonsense, his mother said a few inches away. She crawled out of the doghouse, which would've been impossible when she was still alive, on account of her missing hands. Diabetes had not treated her kindly. What had started as a hangnail had become infected, turned gangrenous so that the surgeons were forced to remove both hands within six months of each other. She shushed him, even though he hadn't spoken aloud. *You're the least crazy person I know, dear.*

"Says my dead mother."

You always did have a good sense of humor. You got that from your father. You two would have gotten on just fine. Pity you never met.

He rubbed his eyes. "I need to get out of this fucking town."

Not until you take your medicine and bring that girl back to her mother.

He shook his head, wiped away sweat that had chilled in the cold breeze. "No more medicine. I'm okay. I've always been okay. You may find this hard to believe but *you* were the one that was sick. Sick in the head."

Maybe so but now's not the time to be pointing fingers. And besides, you look pale. Are you coming down with something?

He scooted away from her and pulled out the

56

bottle of blood-like syrup, downing three quick sips. Not because he feared she was right but because it was the only thing that seemed to make her go away. Ironic if you thought about it hard enough. But Briggs didn't want to think anymore tonight. He wanted to go back to the one-star pirate motel and get some sleep. He belched and stood up just as his mother melted into thin air.

He checked both ways for pig monsters before crossing the street.

✱✱✱

"What happened to your face?" Michelle said.

"Long story," Liam said, still whispering. They stood in the living room of his apartment, lights off, shades drawn. Pitch black inside, her breath on his neck. He reassured himself it wasn't something large and beastly. It wasn't about to open its jaws and snap into his flesh.

He slid his fingers into the rungs of the blind and looked outside. Nothing but a neighborhood cat and a few cars driving by. It didn't feel that way, though. It felt like the moment he stopped watching was the moment that *thing* would crawl out of the bushes and make its way up the stairs.

He slid the extra chain on the door into place for good measure.

"What was that thing?" Michelle said, following him like a concerned puppy.

"Hell if I know."

"Why was it chasing you?"

"Do you always ask this many questions?" He looked outside again. Nothing. For the moment.

"Only when I have near-death experiences."

He sighed, breathing steadily for the first time since Flanagan's. She was probably just as scared and he was giving her a hard time. "I'm sorry. I didn't mean to snap. I guess I get cranky when *I* have near-death experiences."

"That's okay. I'm used to you being cranky."

He raised his eyebrows.

"You're not exactly the nicest customer. You looked like you were going to stab me today when I asked about your script."

It was meant as a joke but he didn't like the analogy. The thought of sharp things digging into skin did no favors for his nerves. "Sorry about that too."

"Water under the bridge. Is this your place? It's pretty rad." She turned on the lights.

He nearly screamed. "What the hell are you doing? Turn those back off, will you?"

She waved him off. "It's gone now, whatever it was. Probably a bear or something."

"A bear? You can't be serious."

She didn't answer him.

The framed picture of Heather, still on his bedside table, watched him, rolling her eyes. It was the look she'd always given him that said *you're pathetic and I want you to know it.*

Michelle looked through his things, lifting movies and reading their descriptions. She studied the wall of posters. Her eyes narrowed in on the Clive Sherman autograph. "I noticed your t-shirt but I didn't know you were the stalker type."

He looked at the image on the front of his shirt. *The Blonde Bimbo Massacre* cover art was smudged with dirt and blood. "I'm not a stalker just because I have an autograph."

"Whatever you say. I've heard he's a fucking prick. If I were you, I'd take it down. Put up a picture of a naked zombie chick or something." Her tone had changed too quickly, from playful to spiteful. She moved closer to it, examined Clive's smug face. In the picture he held a severed arm prop, bone peeking from the gore-soaked side. She shook her head in disgust.

"You're right about that." Liam grabbed two beers from the fridge, handing her one. They cracked them open in unison. "He's the reason I look like the elephant man. Bastard cold-cocked me tonight." He held the chilled can against his jaw and hissed through his teeth. It only seemed to make the pain worse.

Michelle spun around as if she'd just been told she hit the lottery. Her eyes were wide and she gulped the beer quickly, some of the froth sticking to her upper lip. He noticed again how good she looked this close up. Even more so now that she was in his apartment. "What did you just say?"

He nodded. "That's right. He *is* a prick and he's in town, believe it or not. He bought my place of employment like it was nothing and now I have one hundred dollars to my name. He fished the crumpled check from his pocket and tossed it onto the coffee table.

"You mean you actually met him? Did he say where he was staying or how long he'd be in town?"

Liam held up his hands to calm her. "I thought you said you weren't a fan."

She looked at the autograph again. "I'm not." She paused. "I just . . . it's odd having a celebrity in town. If you consider him a celebrity. Maybe you could help me find him."

"I'm never going near that man again." One of the cuts along his chin had started to itch. He didn't dare scratch the wound for fear that it would start bleeding again.

"What's the matter? Baby got a boo boo?" Just like that the anger was gone, switched off, turning the mocking meter all the way up instead. Without knowing what it meant, Liam realized she was hiding something.

"And what about the guy that chased you? You want to tell me what that was about?"

"I told you everything already. I got off work and he was waiting for me. Thanks again, by the way. For saving me."

She smiled and his stomach tightened. Maybe it was the beer or the adrenaline or almost getting eaten, but this girl, with her dreadlocks and tattoo and go-fuck-yourself attitude, was making him nervous. In a good way. She was the polar opposite of Heather.

She finished her beer and tossed the can in the sink. "Do you mind if I stay here tonight?"

He opened his mouth but nothing came out. His jaw ached from the motion and his mind offered no words. Did she mean *stay* as in she wanted to *sleep* with him? Of course she didn't. Right? His heart jack-hammered against his ribs. He hadn't *been* with anyone since Heather—or before, for that matter. The thought of seeing another girl naked seemed sacrilegious. But why should he care? Heather had left him high and dry and though he'd daydreamed of her return countless times, the cold, hard truth was that she was gone for good.

Michelle curled a dreadlock in her fingers. "Look, don't get all pervy on me. You're a cute guy and you seem nice enough but I'm not looking for a one-night stand. I'm tired and cranky and I'd like to sleep next to someone tonight, considering recent events. That okay with you?"

He nodded too quickly, relieved and disappointed at once.

She walked toward the futon in the living room, kicked off her shoes and socks, undid her zipper and slid her jeans off. She reached into her sleeves and unclasped her bra in one expert motion, tossing it to the floor. He tried not to stare at her ass but there was no getting around it.

"Stop drooling and come to bed. Unless you'd rather sleep on the floor. That's fine by me."

She slid beneath the covers and lifted the picture of Heather from the neighboring table. "This your girlfriend or something?"

"Ex."

"And you still have her picture watching you sleep at night? You sure you're not a stalker?"

"I just . . . I meant to put it away but I haven't gotten around to it yet. It's not a big deal."

She set it back down and laughed. "Relax. I didn't mean anything by it. She's pretty. But do you mind if I turn her around for tonight? She's trying a little too hard with that smile and she kind of gives me the creeps. Which I don't need any more of tonight."

"Not at all." But part of him, the part that Heather had manipulated so many times he couldn't count, *did* mind. He told that part to shut its mouth.

Michelle spun the frame around so that Heather was staring at the wall. She patted the spot on the cushion beside her.

Liam turned away, took off his jeans and shirt. He

slid beneath the covers and stared at the ceiling, trying to think about anything else but Michelle. He considered getting up and checking the locks again. She reached over, resting her warm and smooth arm over his chest. He could feel her legs against his. They radiated with heat. She smelled sweaty and earthy. He willed himself not to get a hard-on but his body went against his wishes. He wondered if she noticed. If she did she gave no indication.

She yawned and stretched. "You sure you don't want to help me find that prick director? Maybe I can grab an autograph and sell it online. Some weirdo will buy it."

"Not a chance."

"Fine. Maybe I'll have to find him on my own."

"Good luck with that."

IZZY WAS EXPECTING a hotel or maybe a condo, not a haunted house. At least it *looked* haunted. Peeling paint and warped wood and a roof that was ready to topple at any moment. She knew the budget was low, that the crew couldn't afford luxurious lodging, but this place was surely condemned.

The film's director—Clive, as she'd learned on the walk away from the beach—had driven past the waterfront and the shops, farther still through more residential areas, until trees were more abundant than houses. Internal warnings spouted through her mind with each mile. *This guy's bringing you into the woods to fuck and kill you or maybe the other way around.*

She fidgeted in her seat. Clive's hands were clutched tightly around the wheel, his eyes never leaving the road. "It's not much longer."

She nodded, thinking of her escape plan but then

telling herself she was being stupid. This was an opportunity and she should make the best of it. Sooner or later she'd need to go back home to Mommy and Daddy where she'd be grounded for an inconceivable length of time. She ought to enjoy herself a little before then.

Clive turned off the country road onto an unpaved trail leading straight into the woods. The darkness came quickly. Despite the sunlight above, the branches obscured much of the sky.

The path turned rockier, more uneven, until it finally straightened out and ended at a small clearing, overgrown grass reaching knee-high. In the middle of the opening lay the most genuine looking set piece she'd ever seen. A Victorian house, almost as big as her place back home. Dingy windows lined the first and second floors, most of the panes cracked.

Vans and trucks surrounded the place, with piles of equipment that could have been cameras or microphones. Where were the trailers? Where were the people running around and barking orders? It looked more like a redneck convention than a movie set.

Clive parked behind a van with the words *Bone Saw Studios* written across the side doors and cut the engine. He smiled, the gold tooth twinkling even in the dim light. "We're here."

A swinging chair on the porch swayed slowly in the breeze, its rusted chains screeching like hyenas. She did not want to enter those doors.

Too late now, you idiot.

She could make a run for it.

Do you have any idea where you are? When's the last time you were in the woods? You'd die before you made it back to the road.

"You coming or what?" Clive said, propping open the decrepit door.

She nodded and smiled, her heart thumping much too fast.

The interior was even worse. Wallpaper hung in strips, like the walls were shedding dead skin. The large front staircase was warped, the wood splintered. More equipment was set up in the foyer, a makeshift editing booth of some sort. Shadows moved about like they were more than just darkness. Like they could reach out and bite.

"I'll show you to your room," Clive said, climbing the stairs.

A man covered in tattoos stepped out of a doorway upstairs and leaned over the railing. "Boss, I think we're ready to film the beach scene." He looked at Izzy and back at Clive, winking. "Were you going to come along?"

"I'd rather not. Shoot this one without me. Make it look good." He turned toward Izzy and nodded. "CJ, this is Izzy. She's our newest cast member."

CJ nearly drooled. She wished she'd worn something less revealing than her tank top and shorts. She could feel his eyes on her breasts like slimy fingers. She stepped to the side of the stairs farthest away from him as she climbed.

"Nice to meet you," he said.

"CJ, did you have anything else you wanted to ask me?" Clive gritted his teeth.

CJ shook his head. "Sorry, no. That's about it. We'll get going. The special effects are in the van, if you catch my meaning."

Clive reached the top of the stairs. He stopped for a moment to rest, breathing too fast. "I catch it just fine. Now get to it."

"You got it." He ran down the stairs, turned around once at the bottom to take a final glance at Izzy, and headed outside. She wanted to feel relieved now that he was gone but her pulse did not slow.

"Here's your room," Clive said, down the left hall now, outside the last door on the left.

The stairs were just behind her. She could still make a run for it. This guy seemed nice enough but there was one obvious point. He was hiding something. He *was* a director. He hadn't lied about that. But there was something else. Something that got under her skin and made her want to spring in the direction they'd came.

Stop being a wuss. Isn't this why you came out here in the first place? To rebel? Well, what are you waiting for? It doesn't get any more rebellious than this.

She nodded, more to herself than Clive. From here on she was going to take life as it came. She'd survived two months on her own, had slept in a broken down van on most nights. She could make it through a week or two of shooting a low-budget gore fest.

"It's not much," Clive said. "We don't have any fancy amenities but this place has a roof and working plumbing and that's more than I can say about some of the other places we've stayed at."

"It's fine. Really. I'm just happy to be part of the movie."

"That makes two of us. Let's get you settled."

The first thing she noticed was how dark the place was. Darker than it should have been. Granted the light was off but something else was missing too. No windows of any kind, like they'd been boarded over. She held the wall for support and her hand touched something warm and soft, like foam. Before she could question her surroundings, Clive turned on the light.

Her eyes took in everything in steps. She'd been right about the windows. Two-by-fours had been nailed over the frames. The material she'd touched was indeed foam, stapled to the walls, hanging in ridges like something you'd find in a recording studio. Like it was meant to soundproof the room.

On the floor in the far corner lay a dirty mattress, springs cutting through the fabric's surface in several places. There were more stains along the material than she could count. But none of these things made her want to scream more than the three girls that were huddled together. Their hands and mouths were bound and they whimpered like lost puppies. Izzy got the sense they'd been here for a long time.

Clive pushed her forward and she lost her balance, falling to the floor and hitting her forehead on the way down. The world turned from pitch black to blinding white. Then Clive was on top of her. He grabbed her hands, held them together, and tied something rough around them. A zip-tie, she realized. The sudden pressure on her wrists sent pins and needles through her skin. Next he grabbed a roll of duct tape and ripped off a generous strip with his teeth, placed it over her mouth. It took great effort to move. Blood dripped from the spot where she'd hit her forehead.

"It's nothing personal," Clive said. "What I said back at the beach, about you having guts? I meant every word of it. And we'll need those guts during filming." He smiled and his tooth twinkled once more, like it was smiling along with him. "Try and get some sleep. It's going to be a long couple of days."

***

Later that night, Clive travelled the overgrown path behind the house and retired to his shack. The view was breathtaking. You could see the ocean through the branches if you squinted and the sprawl of the landscape sometimes gave him chills.

But tonight it was too dark to see much. Tonight he had the chills for a different reason. The sky had clouded over and the moon was dim. He drank cheap whisky straight from the bottle and didn't notice the burning sensation as it slid into his belly.

His movie was shit. He'd known that going in, of course. Most of his movies were shit but they radiated a certain charm. He'd always taken pride in them, could see through their flaws. They wore their weaknesses on their sleeves. This one, though, was quite the opposite. The script, in simple terms, was nonexistent. As was the plot. Take for example the scene CJ had filmed at the beach earlier that night. Why the hell would Pigfoot bury a hobo in the sand before crushing his face to a pulp? It didn't make sense. None of this did.

But he couldn't dwell on it. The movie was out of his hands, had been since he'd made a certain promise to a certain someone who had promised something in return.

The door to his shack creaked open. It could have been the wind but he knew better. He could feel a presence there, watching him, smiling as it slid forward and stood just behind him. Cold air on his flesh, breath that did not belong to the living. It still made him shiver after all this time.

"You're having second thoughts," it said.

He nodded. "I guess I am."

"It's too late for that sort of thing." Its voice was mathematically impossible, never settling on a single pitch or tone. It defied physics and just about everything Clive knew to be rational.

"I'm not backing out if that's what you're worried about. I'm in it for the long run. Just like we discussed."

It placed a cold hand on his shoulder and for a moment his body came alive. Then the fantasy broke and he was back in this rundown shack behind the rundown house in this shithole town and he was still about to sell his soul to the devil.

Tara was nude, as she always was. It seemed ludicrous to imagine her clothed, as if she'd transform into something else entirely with even a single glove on her hand. Her flesh was pale in the night, giving off a faint glow. She was equally beautiful and horrifying, exactly how he'd imagined when he'd written her into the original script. But she'd changed the script since then, had given him numerous notes and infinite power.

He saw it all again, was back in these woods, location scouting. This was to be his final film, an awful Pigfoot sequel that would end the series with a bang—literally. The beast was going to procreate and there would be tiny piggy monsters taking over the world. He'd been deep in thought, thinking about all the ways he could kill off the main stars, when his foot gave out and he fell through a layer of leaves into a six-foot hole not unlike a grave. Whoever had dug it, some hunter or redneck, had taken great care. You wouldn't have noticed the opening unless you knew its exact location. That wasn't the worst part, though.

The worst part was the way his ankle bone jutted out of the skin at an angle that defied the laws of nature almost as much as Tara.

Blood spouted from the new opening like a garden hose. He began to feel light-headed and cold. He was going to die in a hole, deep in the woods of a New England tourist trap. His undeserving ex-wife would get the rest of his money—and there wasn't a whole lot to give—and by the time anyone found his body, he'd be a skeleton, a prop in his own movie.

He imagined, as stupid as it was, that Tara would come to his rescue. In the script, she was the main starlet: tough as nails and hot as hell. She had perfect tits and a knack for killing mutant pigs. She was everything he wanted in a woman, someone who could fuck your brains out and knock your lights out at the same time.

He imagined slender fingers appearing along the edge of the hole, giving way to a tanned wrist and so forth until the most beautiful creature he'd ever known appeared. An earthworm crawled across the surface and a squirrel leapt from a branch. No Tara. No rescue.

He sighed and prepared to die.

And heard a noise.

Faint at first, could have been a trick of his ears and slowing pulse, but the feeling in his gut was enough to make him tense up. Someone rustled through leaves above.

You're going crazy. It's just the wind. You're going to die alone and there's not a whole lot that can change that.

The breeze picked up and every inch of his skin came alive with a buzzing sensation, like he was being watched from all angles. "Hello?" His voice croaked.

A shadow appeared near the mouth of the hole. He could just make out the shape of someone above, momentarily blocking out the sun, but his vision was fading quickly. "Help. I need help."

The shape nodded. "Yes."

The voice sounded wrong, neither male nor female, nor entirely human.

You're hallucinating. There's no one there.

"I can help you," the shape said. "Is that what you want?"

He tried to nod but his neck was too stiff. The pain in his ankle was taking over, his body going into shock. He opened his jaw as far as it would go and clicked his tongue.

"If I save you," the shape said, "I will expect something in return. Do you understand?"

He clicked his tongue again. *Once for yes, twice for no.* He could have laughed if he wasn't dying.

"Things will be different." The shape's voice was hypnotizing. Everything else faded as if he'd entered a deep and dark tunnel. "You will owe me everything but it will be worth it in the end. I can give you power. I can give you anything you've ever dreamed of, so long as you use that power as I say. Would you like that, Clive? Would you like to have power?"

He had one foot—*ha!*—out the door now, too weak to wonder how she knew his name. And when had the voice taken on a gender? It went from monstrous to elegant in the span of a nanosecond. He used every bit of remaining strength to mouth one simple word.

"Yes."

Blackness then. Deep and infinite for what

seemed like eons. He had the sensation of falling, like the bottom of the hole had given way to an even larger one, an infinite pit with no bottom. Eventually he woke, thinking he was either in heaven or hell but he suspected the first option when he saw who was standing above him, naked as the day she'd been born.

He rubbed his eyes and pinched his skin but the image remained perfectly clear.

Tara. From the script.

He smiled, realizing he was alive, that he could feel the wind on his skin. The pain in his ankle was gone. He touched the flesh and felt smooth skin instead of broken bone. A miracle.

He laughed now, back in the shed, head spinning from the cheap booze. "A miracle my ass."

"What did you say?" Tara asked.

"Nothing. Just thinking out loud."

"I saved you. You would do well not to forget that."

"How could I?" Another swig of whiskey, a monstrous belch. "It's not as if you'd ever let me. I'm a glorified slave. You think I like killing these people? I'm a bastard. There's no denying that. But I'm not a monster."

She ran a cold tongue along his ear lobe. "We both know that's a lie."

"If I'm going to be a murderer, it ought to be on my own terms."

She wrapped her arms around him. His skin warmed despite her frigid fingers. "These *are* your own terms. I got the ideas from you. All of them. I went inside that head of yours and pulled them out, made them possible. I'm just helping you do what you've always wanted. Isn't that right?"

He wanted to tell her she was wrong, that he wasn't a psychopath, but his mouth remained closed as she massaged his scalp with one hand, the other traveling below his belt line. "Yes," he finally managed to say.

"Good. Now rest up. We've got a busy day tomorrow."

The sudden absence of her hands disoriented him, as if he'd woken up in the hole once more.

Tara was gone, though she never felt more than a step away. She had a knack for following you wherever you went.

He supposed that came with the territory.

She did own his soul, after all.

HEATHER WAS BACK.

She'd decided she couldn't live without Liam. She'd been stupid to leave him. Sure, he was a dropout, a loser, a nerd content to live his life without ever reaching his full potential, but he was *her* nerd and she loved him deeply. He wanted to tell her he'd known she would come back but instead he gave into her embrace, felt her fingers trace lines on his chest, working their way down until they ended just below his waist.

Then there was a warmth that seemed infinite as she parted her lips and took him into her mouth.

And bit his dick off with a quick snap of her jaw, blood dripping down her chin as she smiled and chewed.

Liam screamed and rolled off the bed. He looked between his legs and could have cried at the sight of his fully in-tact genitals, wiped sweaty hair from his face and remembered that Michelle had slept over.

He risked a glance toward the bed but it was empty. She'd ducked out early, probably had to work the morning shift. The clock read noon. For a moment he worried he'd be late for his own shift but then remembered he was unemployed as of yesterday.

What the hell was he supposed to do? Go look for a job? There was nothing else he wanted to do in Bass Falls. A tourist shop was out of the question and so was a restaurant. Manual labor and Liam didn't mix well.

He did the next best thing. Pushed aside his current predicament. Pushed aside last night's events, his run-in with Clive, his swollen jaw, his escape from . . . whatever had chased him—all of it. Instead he made a pot of coffee and decided to work on his script.

He'd made several short films, most of them with his friends, though Corey had become harder to cast once Jacquelyn came into in the picture, but this would be his first feature. It had scope and heart and gore and he would be damned if he gave up on the thing.

The poster of Clive watched him write, silently criticizing, his gold tooth like a middle finger.

Did you even finish school?

Liam shook his head. "No, I didn't. And you know what? That's okay. It was filled with hacks and wannabes. I may be a loser but at least I know who I am. And you? You might be a legend but you're still a fucking asshole." He ripped the frame from the wall and tossed it across the room. It collided with the fridge with a satisfying crack.

He ought to do the same with Heather's photo but his dream was still too fresh in his mind. Baby steps.

He finished his first cup of coffee, took two aspirin

in hopes that his jaw ache would recede, and sat down at the kitchen table to work on the script. Usually, in one sitting, he got through a page or two, making countless corrections—long-hand, mind you—but today he managed a total of twenty pages in one hour. The fastest he'd ever worked. His crappy apartment drifted away so that there was nothing else aside from him and the scribbled words on the page. Violence became art. Every drop of blood spilled was something beautiful. The dialogue flowed effortlessly. He wished it could always be like this. Wished he'd never be interrupted again.

Wished all this as the doorbell rang.

Fucker. He ignored it. Maybe whoever was down there would take the hint. Probably just his aunt bugging him for the rent check. Or maybe it was Corey, here to bum some weed off of him, though he'd run out a few days ago.

Or maybe it's that thing that chased you last night. Maybe it remembered your place after all and it's come back to finish what it started.

No. It hadn't been a *thing.* It had been a person, some crazy guy or gal tripping on God knew what.

It sure didn't sound like a person. And if you're so certain, why don't you go on down there and see for yourself?

The doorbell rang again. He walked slowly toward the window, moving aside the curtain and preparing to see some furry thing, impossibly tall and hungry.

But there was no beast outside, only a man with a receding hairline and dark bags under his eyes. He pulled a bottle from his pocket. Filled with something bright red, nearly glowing. The man took three large gulps, whispered something to himself, as if he had an imaginary friend. He belched and rang the doorbell for a third time.

Liam gave in and went downstairs.

This close the man looked sickly. Pale, yellowed skin, oil and sweat hanging onto his pores for dear life. Lips dry and peeling, teeth an uncanny shade of orange. He wore a stained shirt that may have once been white.

"Afternoon," he said.

Liam nodded. "Afternoon."

"I was wondering if I could have a few moments of your time."

"Are you a Jehovah's Witness or something?

The man shook his head. "No, nothing like that."

"Then what exactly?"

"I'd like to discuss a private matter." He smiled, looking to his left.

"Are you a salesman?" Liam stepped back. There was something off about the man, something that didn't scream "stable."

"Do I look like a salesman to you?"

"I guess not."

"Now, do you have a second or what?" The corners of his mouth were stained red from whatever had been in the bottle.

"I was actually on my way out," Liam said too quickly.

"Bullshit."

Liam offered a nervous smile. "It was great talking to you but I've really got to be going. Have a good day." He made to shut the door but the guy blocked it with his arm.

"What do you know about Maura Black?"

"Who?"

"Don't play dumb. The girl who stayed here last night and took off early this morning."

Alarms bells rang through Liam's head. *This guy has been watching you. He's a cop or something, maybe undercover. Or maybe he's a stalker. Hell, he's the bastard that chased Michelle last night. He ought to do his homework. He thinks she's someone else.* "I don't know what you're talking about."

"Look, this would be a hell of a lot easier if you'd just come out with it. It would save us both the trouble." He scratched his hair furiously as if lice had long ago laid eggs on his scalp.

"There was no girl here last night. Do I look like the kind of guy that has girls over?"

"I don't care what kind of guy you are. Maura Black was here last night and I need to speak with her. It's an urgent matter."

"If I run into someone by that name, I'll be sure to pass on the message." He tried to close the door again but the man kept his arm in place.

"Boy, that girl is playing you like a fiddle. If you really think her name is Michelle, you ought to hear me out."

"And you ought to turn around and head back to your car, maybe drink another bottle of cough syrup. I told you she wasn't here and I meant it. Now if you don't get out of here in ten seconds I'm going to call the cops and something tells me you don't want that." He tried his best to sound tough, gritted his teeth and stared the guy in the eyes. Heather would've been proud.

The man sighed and finally let go of the door. "A word of advice. If I were you I'd think twice about shacking up with her again. She's hiding something— aside from her identity. I'm not sure what but I intend to find out." He turned and walked toward the street, mumbling to himself or his invisible friend.

✶✶✶

Michelle wasn't behind the counter. Perhaps she was out back cleaning or maybe she'd taken her break. Once it was Liam's turn to order he asked for a large coffee from a man with a beard and Coke bottle glasses. "Do you know where Michelle is?" he asked, tapping his fingers on the counter.

The man looked up as he put a lid on the cup. "You mean the girl with the dreadlocks?"

Liam nodded, took his coffee and paid.

The man rang him out, his eyes magnified like a funhouse mirror through the thick lenses. "You know her?"

"I wouldn't be asking if I didn't." He laughed, hoping to lighten the mood. The guy seemed tense all of a sudden.

"Then you can tell her she's fired. I don't care if she's sick or hung over or dead, to be honest. We have a zero tolerance policy with no-call, no-shows. Let her know she can pick her last paycheck up here. She never filled out any paperwork when we hired her. No address on file. I should start being more rigid about these things but it's cheaper to pay under the table." His glasses started to droop, making his eyes seem half the size.

Liam thanked him and left. Outside he winced at the sudden sunlight. Something didn't add up. He'd thought she was hiding something last night, while she sneered at the picture of Clive Sherman. When you threw the stalker from this morning into the mix, the equation grew much more complicated.

He didn't have her address or phone number. His only link had been the coffee shop and now that thread was severed. How the hell was he going to find her?

His cell phone rang from within his pocket. There was no name on the screen and he didn't recognize the number. He thought about letting it go to voicemail but answered instead. "Hello?"

A pause. "Liam?"

"Yeah?"

"Hey, it's Michelle."

"You must be psychic."

"Sorry I cut out early this morning. I had work." He looked through the windows at her angry boss wiping the counter and shaking his head in disgust at something. "I looked through your phone before I left and saved your number. Hope you don't mind. I wasn't trying to be creepy. I swear."

"It's okay. I don't mind."

"Good. Listen, I was thinking. Did you maybe want to hang out tonight? Watch a movie or something? Maybe grab a drink?"

Something made him pause. What if she really *wasn't* Michelle? What if she *was* someone named Maura Black? Then he remembered her warmth and how lonely he'd felt this past year. "That sounds great. Does seven work?"

"Make it eight. I'll meet you at your place." She hung up.

He put his cell back in his pocket and started walking. From the corner of his eye, he saw a familiar Buick drive by slowly and turn the corner.

***

"Isn't that cute." Briggs watched the kid speed up. "He's trying to get away. Maybe he forgot I know where he lives." He kept his distance just the same, didn't need a hit and run on his record. He wanted to finish up this case as smoothly as possible.

"Roll up the window," his mother said. "You're going to catch cold."

"It's ninety-three degrees out. I think I'll be fine." The perspiration felt like tiny icicles, a combination of the temperature and withdrawals from his medicine. It had only been an hour since his last dose. He'd already gone through half a bottle since waking. He was getting worse.

"Then put on the air conditioner. You don't want to faint."

"So I'll either catch something or faint but there's no in-between? Besides, it's broken."

She sighed. "You're going to get yourself sick, end up bed-ridden, and it's going to be the death of me."

He could have laughed if it were under different circumstances. Say, for example, if his mother wasn't five years in the ground and he wasn't losing his mind. "For the last time, you're not real and even if you were, I'm not the one who's sick. How many times do we have to go through this?"

"You think just because a bunch of doctors thought it was odd that I liked to take care of my son, make sure he recovered from all his illnesses, that I was sick? I wanted a healthy boy and there's nothing sick about that. If you had any kids you'd understand. You should find yourself a wife and settle down. It's not too late, you know."

Briggs rolled his eyes and turned left, following the kid toward wherever his destination was. He tried to block out his mother's droning voice, which was no easy feat. It went on and on about infections and bacteria and how the common cold was nothing to laugh about. There was nothing wrong with taking precautions here and there.

Precautions? Is that what they were? Because he seemed to remember it differently. He remembered her shaving his head because of invisible lice. He remembered her taking his temperature in every orifice several times a day just to make sure he wasn't running a fever. He remembered her shoving a penlight into his eyes and ears and mouth, looking for hidden pustules and tumors. And how could he forget the Visine he'd caught her slipping into his cereal or the Windex she'd sprayed into his cocoa? When she couldn't find anything wrong with her healthy boy, she'd resorted to making him sick. Because then she could take care of him. Then she could feel needed and wanted. She could be the hero, the mother who took care of her son and nursed him back to health.

And the irony of it all, she'd been so worried about her son that she hadn't bothered to take care of herself. She'd eaten nothing but junk food, drank nothing but soda, until her pancreas protested. The diabetes came on strong, wreaked havoc on her circulation so that paper cuts turned to infections, which turned to gangrene, which turned to rotting flesh. She lost the tips of fingers and then the fingers themselves, followed finally by the hands until she was a fraction of the woman she'd once been, unable to feed or clean herself.

Until Briggs had been unable to see her like that anymore.

He'd made a choice one night, while the nurses in the rehab center were too busy texting instead of checking on that poor woman in room thirty-two.

"Are you even listening?" his mother said.

Briggs blinked and he was about to hit a parked car. He jerked the wheel and noticed that he'd lost the kid. Tonight, he'd have to stake out that shitty apartment again and hope that Maura returned.

"Watch where you're driving." His mother tisk tisked him and went back to her speech about the importance of cleaning your hands properly. Did you know bacteria could stay under your nails for up to one month? A month! Did you really want that stuff living under there, making its way into your body when you weren't paying attention?

He opened a fresh bottle of cough syrup and wondered if there was an end to this. Not his assignment or his current line of work but his other predicament, the one sitting inches away from him. He took several generous gulps of the syrup and his dead mother faded to nothingness. Lunch and coffee were in order.

He had a long night ahead of him.

SCOTTY ALLEN WAS too excited to question anything that had happened over the last two days. Sure, it seemed odd that Clive Sherman, grindhouse and gore extraordinaire according to Liam, would cut him a generous check to close down his shop. It seemed even weirder that Clive had been adamant about Scotty not cashing the check until they'd finalized the deal. Not that he was complaining.

The only remaining step in the transaction was to meet Clive and his associates at the store and hand over the keys, maybe sign a few documents. Then Scotty could be on his way to retirement. He could move out of his cramped apartment, which was straight out of the seventies and always smelled of cigarette smoke, though he'd never smoked a day in his life. He could move closer to Boston, buy a moderately priced condo, and live the rest of his life in hermit glory. No interaction with customers, only the occasional night out with acquaintances, and all the movie theaters and buttered popcorn he desired. It all sounded too heavenly to question.

If Scotty did have a nagging voice inside his head, it would've been screeching at full volume as he parked along the curb outside Roger Street Video Rental. The front door was open. He cut the engine and looked at the shop's key in his hand, the gears in his head turning, albeit slowly. The windows had been boarded over. The light within the doorway seemed dim but he could see shapes moving around, could make out piles of camera equipment.

He smiled like an idiot and got out of the car, tasting the salty essence of popcorn and the high fructose corn syrup of a mega-sized Slurpee. Almost there. Just a few forms to fill out and that was all.

He marched through the open door like the happiest man on earth.

Clive Sherman was speaking to one of his crewmembers. The guy, covered in tattoos, nodded toward the entrance. Clive turned around and smiled toward Scotty, his gold tooth twinkling. He came over and held out his hand. Though the director seemed confident, there was something else in his eyes too. They had a tired and weary look, like he hadn't slept in a very long time. Like he was spooked by something.

Scotty shook the man's hand. "Nice to see you again, Mr. Sherman."

"You too, son. I can't thank you enough for allowing us to store our things here. You can't imagine how big of a help you've been." He squeezed Scotty's hand a bit too hard before letting go.

"Don't mention it. When I realized who you were,

I couldn't believe it. We had all your movies in the shop. Even the lesser known ones. Hell, one of my best employees, Liam, is obsessed with you. Wears your shirts all the time like a uniform."

Clive scratched at grey stubble along his cheek. It sounded like knives being sharpened. "You know what? I think I might've met your friend last night. Short kid, maybe this high?" He held a hand to his shoulder. "Shaggy hair, was wearing a *Blonde Bimbo Massacre* t-shirt that had seen better days."

Scotty nodded quickly, beaming. "That's him. I'm so glad he got to meet you."

"The pleasure was all mine. Seemed like a nice kid."

Scotty kept nodding, unsure of what else to say. His mind was too busy fantasizing about never again waking to the sound of an alarm clock, eating piles of candy while he watched the biggest television that Best Buy carried. "I guess you'll need this," he finally said, holding out the key to the shop. His nonexistent inner monologue would've screamed its lungs out at that moment. *What's the point, you fat fuck? They're already in here. Can't you smell something fishy when it's right in front of your nose?*

Clive took the key, spun the ring around his finger a few times, and placed it into his pocket. "Thanks. And the check? Like we discussed, you didn't cash it yet?"

Scotty shook his head and pulled it out of his wallet. "Uncashed just like you asked."

"Perfect. Scotty." He snapped his fingers at a couple crewmembers. "Boys, can you get the doors?"

They stopped what they were doing and giggled like teenagers about to see their first pair of breasts.

Practically skipped toward the doors and shut them, turning on the rest of the lights.

Scotty hadn't noticed the cameras before. They rested on tripods and pointed in his direction. One of the crewmembers turned on two professional grade lights and Scotty was momentarily blinded. From his left he noticed a man approaching from what had been the porn section. He carried a boom mike and asked Clive if they were good to go.

"Not yet," Clive said. "There's one more thing." He grabbed Scotty's wrists and pulled the check from his fingers. He held the slip of paper close to Scotty's eyes, which were now adjusting to the light, and tore it into several pieces. "You know the funniest part? Other than you believing all of this? The check isn't even real. If you'd tried to cash it, they would've laughed in your face. It's as good as Monopoly money."

Per Scotty's doctor's orders he was supposed to carry an inhaler at all times and lose roughly fifty pounds by the year's end. The year was more than half over and he weighed two pounds more than when it had begun. The inhaler was at home, resting next to an empty package of Ramen noodles. "What the hell's going on here?" He sounded even more like a scared child than normal and his wheezing made it hard to breathe.

"What's going on," Clive said, "is that I took advantage of your intelligence. My producer's got me by the balls and she seemed to think you were just the man for the job. We *are* using your shop for storage. That part's true. It's conveniently located only two miles from where we're lodging and close enough to the town center for when we shoot the final act."

"W-w-what's the final act?" He held his throat, breath entering and exiting his lungs in tiny bursts.

"Just like in any good horror flick, the final act is when everything goes to hell. Boys?"

The door to the employee break room burst open. Three shapes stood in the entryway. The first was a bearded man with a tribal-style nose ring. He held some sort of metallic rod. The second was clean-shaven and pale, also holding a rod. The third was not bearded or skinny or a man at all. It was well over six feet tall and its skin was the color of sweet and sour pork. Come to think of it, its face had a distinct pig-like quality and the more Scotty looked at it, the more he realized he'd lost his mind.

Either that or the Pigfoot had somehow stepped out of the world of make-believe and into Bass Falls.

All things considered, the latter theory seemed to make the most sense.

It snorted and struggled. Scotty saw now that the rods were connected to circular rings that secured the thing's neck, meant to keep it in line.

They slid the rings from its head.

"Make sure you clean this place up," Clive said. "Roger, grab the bucket. Get as many of the leftovers as you can. We'll use them later."

Roger, an older man with an obscene gut and a face covered with acne scars, slid over something that looked like a vat of toxic waste. It was filled with red liquid. Things like fingers and eyes floated throughout.

Scotty backed against the front door. He calculated how long it would take to spin around and make his escape. His mind worked much too slowly.

The Pigfoot grabbed his ankles and pulled him to the floor. Bones snapped. Pain seared. His legs tore free. Roger tossed both limbs with the rest of the blood and body parts, special effects that were extra special.

Scotty screamed for what seemed like eons.

Until the Pigfoot reached forth with a hooved hand, ripped his jaw from his face, and tossed it to the blood-soaked floor. He quieted down after that.

And watched as more and more of his body was removed in expert motions.

On the floor, next to a camera lens cap and the torn check, was something that seemed so fitting, so preternaturally *right*, that he stared at the object for the rest of his life, which was roughly fifteen seconds.

It was the sign from yesterday.

Going out of business sale.

I ZZY WORKED AT the duct tape with her tongue for hours. Eventually, just as her jaw hurt too much to move, the strip tore from her lips and the loose end hung down her cheek. Two of the other three girls were still sleeping. Their grimy faces lay at awkward angles on the mattress. The third, a girl who could've been Izzy's age, with blood-red hair that matched the blood-red lacerations on her cheekbones, watched Izzy like a statue. She made no expression, no hint of fear or sadness or pain on her face.

Izzy slid forward and lifted her legs, placing her bound wrists under her bottom and the back of her knees, so that they looped around to the front. She leaned toward the girl's face, and latched onto the rag that blocked her mouth. It took a few tries but the rag came undone and slid downward.

The girl did not shout. Instead she cracked her jaw and lay back against the wall. "Don't bother screaming. It's a waste of time." Her voice was gravelly, spoke of dehydration and hunger. She nodded toward the soundproofing foam. "The last girl that tried that isn't here anymore. We heard her screaming for a while. It must've been pretty loud to get through that stuff."

Hundreds of questions spun through Izzy's head but there was one in particular that shoved itself to the front of the line. "What the fuck is this place?"

The girl did not blink. Her eyes looked just as dry as her tongue. "A haunted house."

"Come again?"

"An old hermit used to live here. Harry Townson, although most people just called him Scary Harry. He was the heir to a make-up company. A weirdo, the kind of guy that stared too much and mumbled to himself. He creeped most people out and started going into town less and less, had this place built with his family's money. They paid him to stay away from civilization. They couldn't have their crazy son messing up their company's image. So he lived here, two miles from the nearest road, had all his food delivered, only left this place a couple times a year at most."

"And where is Harry now?"

"Best I can tell, he's probably dead. This guy, Clive? He found this place while location scouting and took it over. It's genius if you think about it. No one is brave enough to come out here and check on Scary Harry. It's as remote as you can get without being too far from town and it's the perfect place to set up your headquarters."

"Headquarters." The word rested heavily on Izzy's tongue.

"Let me guess. He gave you the movie speech, said you had what it took to be in front of the screen, said the budget was next to nothing but you'd get some exposure and some warm meals."

Izzy nodded, feeling equal parts naïve and stupid.

"He gave us the same spiel. I knew it sounded too good to be true but I fell for it anyway. It's a small town. Nothing ever happens here, you know? So I had him drive me into the woods, walk me into Scary Harry's home. He told me Harry had agreed to the shoot. I believed that son of a bitch every step of the way until he brought me up here. And . . . well, I guess you know the rest." She held up her zip-tied hands.

"So the guy is some kind of perv who kidnaps girls. The movie . . . it's just a front?"

"That's the problem. It *is* real. As real as it gets. See, when he kills someone on screen there aren't any special effects involved. The blood isn't corn syrup and food coloring. It's more of a documentary than anything."

Izzy cried. It wasn't something she did often. She'd been on her own, sleeping in a broken-down car in the woods for two months. She'd put up with white picket fences and the perfect nuclear family for most of her life, all the while smiling and pretending she gave a shit about any of it. But now, in this dirty soundproofed room, in the middle of the woods, surrounded by three bloodied girls, the floodgates finally broke down. Her body heaved with the intensity of her tears. She sobbed and gagged and settled into a fetal position.

It went on like that for a long time before her eyes had cried themselves dry, until she promised herself she was not going to die in this place. No matter how bad things looked. She wiped her nose on her shoulder and sniffled. "So that's it then. He just wants to kill us."

The girl shook her head, a sad smile curving across her face. "No. It gets worse."

"Worse? How the hell could it get any worse?"

"I take it he didn't tell you about the Pigfoot and the script?"

Izzy raised her eyebrows. "Pigfoot? Are you saying he's got some sicko dressed up like a pig and he's having the guy cut people up?"

"No, I'm saying he's got the *real* Pigfoot in a cage downstairs and that he's having it chow down on people while he films the whole thing. Don't ask me how it's possible because I don't have a clue. But I've seen the thing with my own eyes. Clive makes us watch. He says the fear looks more realistic for the camera that way."

"We have to get out of here. There's got to be a way out, right? I mean, maybe one of us can run while the rest of us . . . "

"While the rest of us, what, take on the crew downstairs? We're outnumbered, we're two miles from town, and may I remind you, we're tied up like Christmas presents. We're not going anywhere."

"So that's it? You're just going to give up and let the pig thing—assuming, of course, it isn't just a guy in a latex mask—eat you?" Izzy backed away. Suddenly she felt about as safe in this room as she had out of it.

She thought of a dozen other questions but they faded when footsteps climbed the stairs and approached the door.

The girl closed her eyes and bowed her head. "I told you it got worse."

The door opened.

***

Liam paced his apartment. He had sweat through three shirts thus far and it had nothing to do with the temperature. Michelle was due at his place any moment. He'd cleaned as best he could, threw away empty beer cans, swept up dust bunnies and ashes and the occasional discarded roach. He'd even tucked the pictures of Heather and Clive away in his closet. The former because it felt like she was watching over him, ridiculing him. The latter because he'd seen the way Michelle stared at Clive, noted the fire in her eyes and the sudden change in behavior. Not to mention her practically begging to set up a meet and greet. There was something there, something he couldn't put his finger on. Then there was the matter of the crazy man who'd been asking about her. It didn't take a scientist to realize the two events were related. He felt like the secret was just within his reach. He just needed that final piece of the puzzle and all would be revealed.

Speaking of revealing, he couldn't get his mind off the way she'd looked last night. The fear from his chase had put a damper on things. He hadn't been able to properly process the night. Now that some time had passed, he could not remove from his mind the image of her legs and stomach and everything else. They were burned behind his eyelids like tattoos.

The doorbell rang.

His heart fluttered, stopped for a moment, sped back up. He hadn't felt this way in a long time and that both thrilled him and scared the shit out of him. *You can do this. She's just a girl. A girl who is incredibly attractive and is clearly hiding something.*

Downstairs, he expected to see Michelle's dreadlocks and perfectly placed lip ring.

Instead he saw Corey, his arm around Jacquelyn's shoulders. Behind them Marcus held a thirty-pack of PBR, a bag of weed clearly dangling from his jeans pocket.

"You going to let us in," Jacquelyn said, "or are you going to stand there like an idiot all night?"

Liam nibbled on his lip. "I . . . you . . . what are you guys doing here?"

"It's Friday," Corey said. "You told us to come over last time we hung out."

"Did I? Because I don't remember saying that."

"Well you said it." Jacquelyn spoke between open-mouth smacks of chewing bubble gum.

"Look, I hate to do this but now's really not a good time."

Corey laughed. His eyes were red and blood-shot. One step closer and Liam would get a contact high. "You got a girl up there or something?"

Jacquelyn snorted, blew a giant pink bubble, and popped it with her tongue. "Yeah, right. That would be the day. Romeo lost his Juliet, remember?"

Liam eyed Corey, tried his best to send a psychic message. "No, it's nothing like that. I just . . . "

"Bullshit," Marcus said from the back. "I can see your boner from here. Is she hot?"

Jacquelyn smiled, lips curling into a Cruella de Vil grin. "Well, I'll be damned. He *does* have a girl up there. I guess miracles do come true. Why don't you introduce us?"

Liam opened his mouth to tell his friends, in not so many words, to get lost, when he heard footsteps coming up the drive. Corey, Jacqueline, and Marcus parted like the Red Sea, revealing Michelle. She held a bottle of wine and he thought she was even more beautiful tonight. He'd been a fool to ever think differently, to give her a hard time when she asked about his script. She held the bottle up and nodded toward Marcus's beer. "Nice. I didn't realize we were having a party. I would've brought something classier."

Jacqueline was beaming. "Liam, aren't you going to introduce us to your friend?"

He gritted his teeth, imagined the sound her neck would make as he snapped it. "Michelle, this is Corey, Jacqueline, and Marcus. Guys, this is Michelle."

Jacqueline shook her hand for a bit too long while Corey and Marcus stared at her ass.

Liam tried to think of another way to lose his friends but it was too late. They climbed single-file up the stairs until he was left alone with Jacqueline. She leaned in so that her mouth was near his ear. "Not bad, hot shot. She's got a body on her. I'm going to love every second of tonight. Because I'm going to make you look like a pansy in front of your new little girlfriend if it's the last thing I do."

Before he could respond she climbed the stairs.

He kicked several rocks into the street. The night was ruined. He'd wanted to spend more time with Michelle. *Alone* time. Now he had to put up with that she-devil inside. After a full minute of swearing under his breath he headed for the door.

For just a moment, before he jogged back up the stairs, he had the feeling there was someone else behind him, another uninvited attendee to a party he hadn't planned on having. Only this wasn't anyone he knew. It was someone who wanted to remain hidden.

He spun around and scanned the street but saw nothing.

He certainly *felt* something, though. He felt eyes, hundreds of them, watching his every move. His skin went prickly despite the summer heat.

Then, just as quickly as the feeling had arrived, it went away.

From upstairs he heard the stereo's volume turning up, bottles and cans being opened, and Jacqueline's nasally voice rising to a shrill peak.

"YOU'RE GETTING RUSTY,"** Briggs said to his reflection. "You should've seen this coming. Could've saved a lot of time."

"Don't be so hard on yourself." His mother stood at the bathroom sink, washing her invisible hands. He wondered if she could see the missing digits but then realized he was speculating on a hallucination.

He hadn't looked into the father. Lisa Black had said nothing of her husband. He hadn't thought much of it at the time. She seemed well off and he assumed she was either divorced or married to a lawyer who travelled all the time. The latter theory had been closer to the truth, though the guy certainly wasn't a lawyer.

He'd done some more searching on his not-so-legal software. Something had been eating away at him. He thought back to the bum he'd met on the beach, the one talking about a film director who was in town. He'd dismissed it at the time. The guy was clearly two beers short of a six-pack. But the memory resonated, like he was missing something.

On his way back to the hotel, he'd stopped for a coffee at the nearest gas station and overheard two nerdy looking guys talking about some cult director. They said the guy was in Bass Falls, shooting some movie about blood and guts and a pet pig or something to that effect. The guy was apparently snatching up bums and runaways to star in his production. Briggs recalled hiding behind the bushes last night, as if it was something he could easily forget, overhearing the two men talking about their boss.

Gears turned in his mind.

It took him several times to dial Lisa Black's number correctly. He was overtired and his nerves were shot. His fingers felt like jelly. The phone rang only twice before she answered. He could hear concern in her voice immediately. "Marvin?"

"Briggs. Yes."

"Is everything okay? Please tell me you found my little girl." Her voice slurred badly. He could almost smell the wine from his hotel room.

"I think I may have. She fits the description, looks a lot like the pictures you gave me except she's got dreadlocks and a tattoo and enough piercings to set off a metal detector."

"Yes, she certainly has changed in recent times. It's just a phase. She's trying to express herself, I suppose. I'm not too keen on the way she dresses but she's old enough to make her own decisions."

Is she? Then why'd you hire me to find her for you? "Listen, I have to ask you a question, something you didn't address when we first spoke."

"Anything, so long as you bring my girl home."

He nodded, forgetting for a moment she wasn't in the room with him. His mother watched from the bathroom doorway, her dead face covered with concern. "Is your husband, by any chance, named Clive Sherman?"

A pause. "Yes. No. I mean he *was* my husband. We've been divorced for some time."

"And you didn't think to bring this up?"

"You didn't ask."

He opened his mouth to tell her off but stopped short. She was right. He hadn't asked and that was proof he was losing his edge. He took a sip from his bottle, the thick liquid tasting wonderful as it slid down his throat. His mother shimmered for a moment, like a fading television screen, then evened out, still in the room with him. His necessary dosage was increasing by the day. "Look, from what I've heard, your husband—"

"Ex-husband."

"Right. Your ex-husband happens to be filming a movie in Bass Falls. That seems a bit convenient, don't you think? Considering your girl—who's currently going by the name Michelle, by the way—is out here at the same time."

Another pause, followed by a gasp. "My god."

"You had no idea about this?"

"Of course not. I've tried to keep Maura away from him for a long time. He's . . . well, he's not a good man. To put it lightly."

"Which means your daughter probably didn't come out here to reconnect with him."

"I would think not. She hates him, tells me every chance she can get."

"Then why are they both out here at the same time, Lisa?"

A third and final pause. He thought he heard the sound of gulping in the background. He pictured her draining the rest of the wine and releasing a muffled and courteous belch. "Briggs, there's something you should know. Clive is dangerous. I have scars to prove it. Literal scars. And so does Maura. If you'd gotten a closer look at her tattoo, you'd see that it's warped. Not because it healed poorly but because of the wound *beneath*. He hurt us badly. I let it go on for too long but I was scared and stupid. I hope she isn't planning on doing anything rash."

"That, Mrs. Black, is exactly what I'm driving at."

"What are you saying?"

He licked the last drop from the cough syrup like a famished puppy and tossed the bottle across the room. It ricocheted off the television and landed perfectly in the trash barrel next to the others. "I'm saying that your daughter found out her daddy is in town and I think she wants to teach him a lesson."

✶✶✶

An hour later Briggs was parked outside the kid's house—Liam, according to a cell phone bill in the mailbox. Through the windows, five people laughed and smoked and drank. That was good. He'd wait until they were nice and buzzed and make his move. A girl like Maura, with that sly look in her eyes, and a guy as scummy as Clive—they wouldn't mix well. Especially when you took their family history into account. He'd grab the girl, bring her home, and maybe prevent some bloodshed in the process. Which would give him the edge on raising his rate for this particular assignment.

He yawned and scratched at his stubble, now nearing a beard.

"You should get some sleep," his mother said. "You're exhausted and you're going to get even sicker."

"Not yet," he said, eyes threatening to shut. "I'm almost done with this shithole of a town. Then I'll sleep for a week straight."

He watched as Maura Black came into view through the nearest window, taking a swig from a bottle. For a split second, Briggs longed to be that young again, stupid and reckless instead of middle-aged, noticeably wider, and sitting feet from an apparition.

He reached into the dashboard, grabbed a fresh bottle of medicine, and cracked it open. "Cheers," he said to the window.

THINGS WERE GOING better than Liam had expected. Michelle seemed to get along well with everyone, though Jacqueline still had that evil look on her face. Her eyes sent silent warnings every time he caught her glance. He couldn't tell if it was any more nefarious than her neutral stare.

The thirty-pack was nearly gone and the bottle of wine was down to a few sips. They'd cracked open a bottle of cheap whiskey Liam had been saving for a special occasion. Looking at Michelle and the way she laughed and smiled and fingered a stray dreadlock, he thought this night was just the kind of occasion he'd been waiting for.

The stereo was much too loud, the music switching from rock to rap to metal to pop, neither of them able to settle on a single genre for more than five minutes. It would most certainly wake the neighbors eventually but it was early yet. Liam thought about closing the windows but it was Friday night and the booze coursing through his bloodstream helped curb his worries. His aunt had left earlier that afternoon, as she always did, for the casino. It was twenty miles south of Boston, surrounded by countless bars and shops, a tourist trap of a different kind than Bass Falls. She had a VIP pass, allowing her to stay at a discounted rate every weekend. Which she took full advantage of. No one was going to come knocking on their door tonight.

He hoped.

He glanced quickly outside but saw no one standing there.

From his left he felt a presence akin to whoever or whatever had chased him the night before. He winced as Jacqueline stepped between him and Michelle. She still chewed her gum, despite sipping a beer. "So how did you guys meet?"

He told her to fuck off with his eyes but she didn't seem to get the message.

"We're actually kind of having a conversation," Liam said.

Michelle squeezed his arm. "No, it's okay. I work down at the coffee shop. He's a regular. Always grabs the corner table and works on his script. A little piece of advice: Never ask him what it's about. He might just throw a tantrum on you." She winked at him. His pulse fluttered.

"You'd be surprised how often he throws those tantrums." Jacqueline blew another bubble. It nearly popped before she sucked it back into her mouth. He prayed she would choke on the pink mass. To his knowledge no one in his apartment knew CPR, which was a plus.

"I think you're being too hard on him," Michelle said. It was obvious she wanted out of the conversation but Corey and Marcus were laughing at something on their phones, neither of them able to steal Jacqueline away. *The Evil Dead* was playing on his television, the volume all the way down. It was nearing the infamous tree scene. He wanted to turn the sound up and create a diversion but the remote was across the room. It seemed criminal that no one was watching one of the greatest movies ever filmed.

"That's Liam's problem," Jacqueline said. "He *needs* someone to be hard on him. He needs to toughen up a little. You'd think his skin would be thicker since Heather left him but if anything he's turned into an even bigger sap."

"That's enough, Jacqueline." Liam held up his hand but she ignored the gesture.

"What's the matter, lover boy? You worried this new one will catch on and realize you're a pansy? I noticed you put her picture away." She nodded toward the coffee table. It seemed so bare without the framed image of Heather. "That was mighty brave of you. Maybe Michelle here can make a man out of you yet."

Liam's entire body tensed. Michelle's face was blank. He wondered if she'd be scared away by Jacqueline's warnings. Maybe she realized that he *was* a loser, that he *was* a pansy. Part of him wanted to cry like an infant. *Don't be stupid. That wouldn't help your case any. And besides, did you honestly think a girl like Michelle would go for a guy like you? You really are pathetic.*

He noticed Michelle had started to say something. He shook his head and honed in on her words. " . . . need to lay off, you know? I may not have known him as long as you but I know a good guy when I see one. He's had a rough year and there's nothing criminal in that."

"Wow, I'm impressed," Jacqueline said. "Not as high and mighty as Heather. I'll give you that much. Not as pretty, either. The last one had bigger tits and a better face. Liam, you went from a nine to a four and that's being generous. I'm happy for you. Really. I'm glad you found someone that can tolerate your torture porn and your filthy apartment. She must really dig guys whose parents gave up on them because they're such a burnout."

From the kitchen Corey and Marcus stopped laughing. They no longer eyed their phones.

The music faded. All Liam could hear was his own pulse, throbbing inside his ears. It was impossible to look away from the two girls in front of him, each of them trying to outdo the other's death stare. It was only a matter of time before they grabbed each other's hair and started throwing punches.

Michelle finally opened her mouth and Liam prepared himself for a war cry. But instead of screaming she started to laugh, a chuckle at first but soon it rose to a full-on howl. She wiped a tear from her eye. Had she worn as much make-up as Heather, it would've left a trail of several colors. But her face remained just as perfect. "Am I supposed to feel threatened? Do you think you can intimidate me? Oh, I'm so scared of the big bad bully. I've got news for you, sweetie. Your boyfriend in the other room?" She pointed at Corey, still silent and wide-eyed. "He's going to come to his senses sooner or later and realize he's dating a witch. Then he'll leave and you can move onto the next one. But you know what? No matter how many guys you reel in, they'll be the ones to toss you back into the water. Because girls like you are a dime a dozen and they're not even worth bringing home as a trophy in the long run."

The world turned to slow motion. Everything was painfully clear. Michelle's laughing as it started back up. Corey and Marcus walking from the kitchen to stop what was about to happen. The possessed tree on the screen.

Jacqueline's hand as it wound back and shot forth.

This was it. Jacqueline was going to smack the only girl who'd given Liam the time of day in the last year and Michelle would be scared away for sure. It wasn't worth putting up with this shit for someone as lame as him.

But Michelle dodged the fist at the last moment and pushed Jacqueline forward. She was caught by surprise, tripped over her own feet and tumbled onto her ass, spilling beer onto her expensive clothes that Daddy had most likely purchased. She lay on the carpet for a moment, her mind processing the situation, before she tossed the empty can toward Michelle and stood back up. Corey intercepted her, hauling her back into the kitchen and through the hallway. "I think it's time we get going," he said.

Marcus followed, opening the door to the front yard. The baggy of pot fell from his pocket but he didn't notice. His eyes were plastered toward Jacqueline like he was witnessing an exorcism-in-progress.

She flailed in Corey's arms. "Come over here and say it again, bitch! Bring that rat nest you call hair over so I can scalp you."

Michelle still smiled as she stepped into the front

yard. "Says the girl whose hair color doesn't exist in the real world. You look like a mannequin, sweetheart."

"That's enough, okay?" Corey managed to tear a hand away from his flailing girlfriend and held it up to them. "She's upset and you're making things worse." It was the first time Liam had ever seen his best friend angry. They'd never so much as had an argument. It didn't match the Corey he'd known for so long.

"She's upset?" Michelle said. "Buddy, she started something she couldn't finish and that's my fault? If I were you, I'd get out while you still can. I'd leave—" She stopped speaking suddenly, her eyes drawn elsewhere. Liam followed her line of sight toward the street. A white van was driving by the house. An image graced the side panel: a serrated blade and a severed eye surrounded by neon splattering blood. Under the logo, in neatly printed letters, were the words *Bone Saw Studios*.

Michelle watched the van as a hunter eyes their next potential kill. Her face contorted in anger.

"Is that yours?" she asked Jacqueline, nodding toward the Lexus parked along the curb.

"No, it's my dad's," Jacqueline said from Corey's arms. She still tried to break his grasp but she'd calmed some.

"I need to borrow it." The van was five houses away now.

"Hell no."

"I don't think that's such a good idea." Corey held the keys up. "I'm going to take her home and get her to bed."

"I really need that car," Michelle said.

"Look, I just told you I—"

Michelle kneed him in the crotch. He fell on his side, dropping Jacqueline and cupping his balls as he curled into the fetal position. "Sorry about that," she said as she picked up the keys from the ground.

Marcus snorted with laughter. He was drunk and high out of his mind. He sat down on the dewy grass of the lawn, trying to compose himself.

Michelle opened the driver's side door and slammed it shut, turning on the ignition.

"Go get her!" Jacqueline said. "If she scratches that thing, my dad's going to slaughter me."

Liam peered back and forth between his friends and the Lexus before running toward the street and getting into the passenger seat just as Michelle hit the gas. He watched through the back window. Corey was still hunched over, Marcus was still giggling, and Jacqueline had started to chase after them, waving her hands and spitting out threats. She slowed down to catch her breath after a few moments.

He turned back around, trying to keep his cool. The van turned the corner ahead and Michelle sped up.

"You want to tell me what the hell's going on here?" Liam fumbled with his seatbelt and stepped on a phantom brake as she blew through the stop sign at the end of his street.

"Not really." She concentrated on the road. "It's kind of a long story."

TWO MEN STEPPED into the room that had become Izzy's prison. One of them she recognized as CJ, the creep from last night. This close she saw that his arms and neck were covered with tribal tattoos and that his tongue was surgically forked. He smiled at her and stuck it out, mock-hissing. The other man was shorter and wider with a scar that ran along his cheeks and nose, probably the result of a late-night bar fight. What kind of people was Clive employing for this movie of his?

"Okay, ladies," CJ said. "Time to head downstairs."

The redhead didn't move. She sat perfectly still against the wall, eyes blank and unfocused. The other two, passed out moments before, woke at the sound of CJ's voice and began to scream. Their hair had once been blonde but was now caked with dirt to the point of no return. They resembled each other so closely that Izzy wondered if they were twins. They cried in unison as CJ and the scarred man picked them up and ushered them out of the room.

CJ stood just outside the door, waving his arms. "You girls coming or what." It wasn't a question.

The redhead finally stood and left without a word. Izzy paused, wondering if she could pry the boards from the window. If she broke the glass and jumped from this high, she'd likely break an ankle, maybe two. It would have been worth it if she wasn't so far from the main road.

"You too." CJ stared at her like she was meat and they were taking a trip to the butcher shop.

She followed him down the hall toward the hub of their equipment. Three shapes stood at the foot of the stairs.

The first was Clive, smiling and sipping what smelled like coffee. There was a camera set up in front of him. He studied the girls through the lens as if trying to get the best shot possible. As if this really was just a movie to him.

The second was another girl, only she wasn't covered in filth or blood. She was totally naked. Her skin was pale and her hair was darker than any shade Izzy had ever seen. It seemed to flow on its own accord, melting into the shadows and re-emerging again every few seconds. Izzy had never been attracted to another woman but there was something hypnotizing about this one. It was hard to take her eyes away for fear she'd miss something. *What the hell is this all about?* Izzy thought but her brain stopped working when she caught a glimpse of the third person.

No. Not a *person*. Not a *human*.

It stood well over six feet tall, with slimy pink skin

and a face that was distinctly pig-like. It held the largest pitchfork she'd ever seen, much too life-like to be a prop. Veins bulged from muscular arms. It snorted and licked its lips as it watched CJ escort the girls down the stairs. As crazy as Redhead had sounded, she had not been lying. The Pigfoot was real.

The realization sent Izzy into a mental spasm. She considered all her options as she descended the steps. She could make a run for it. The front door was only feet away. But she was severely outnumbered and her chances of escaping were low to none. She could create a distraction, maybe bite one of the other girls. The twins were still mumbling in fear. If they were to start wailing again, it might buy her enough time to sneak off.

At the bottom step, though, she knew it was pointless to consider escaping. All hope fled when she was inches away from those three figures. She was going to be raped and tortured and then she was going to die a slow death. She wondered where in the movie this scene would fall.

For a nanosecond she imagined her parents stepping through the door to save her. They were probably worried sick, scared to death for their little girl's safety. Weren't they? She thought back to the days before she'd taken off. They'd been growing more and more impatient with her. She'd been lashing out and rebelling and for what? She had two wonderful parents who spoon-fed her, jumped on command. An only child in an upper middle class family she'd grown bored of. So she'd packed her bags one night, thinking she was a badass, thinking she'd play guitar all across America, slum it up for a while. What could possibly go wrong?

The scarred man pushed the twins to the front of the line. The one on the left, slightly shorter, started to cry again. The taller of the two hurled over and puked onto the floor. The Pigfoot's eyes widened. He sniffed the air, dropped the pitchfork, and lapped at the steaming pile like it was fresh feed from a trough. It sent the taller twin into another round of vomiting and the cycle continued. Eventually she stopped heaving and collapsed to her knees.

Clive stepped away from the camera, sipped his coffee and curled his nose. "We really ought to get something better than this crap. It tastes like motor oil. I swear it's half-caff or something. I've had six cups today and I'm just as tired. And I hate being tired." He studied the twins, both on their knees now. "Girls, I really can't thank you enough for agreeing to be in my movie. It means the world to me. I think it's my best yet." He chuckled. "Who am I kidding? It's shit! There's no plot and half of it makes no sense. Hell, yesterday we had ol' Piggy kill a bum who was buried to his head in the sand. Not exactly a cinematic masterpiece. But it holds a special place in my heart. My producer here," he pointed to the naked pale woman, "she promised me it would all make sense in the end. I'll choose to believe her."

"P-please," the twins said in unison. Their tones were harmonized, the sound eerie enough to send Izzy into a fit of shivers.

"See, that's exactly what I want to see in this scene." Clive was pacing now. "I want to see fear. *Real* fear. Shouldn't be hard under these circumstances. Let's run through the scene quickly, shall we? I know you haven't read the script—not that there *is* a script, at least not a physical copy—so I'll make it short. We need to make our day and there are only so many hours left. You girls are going to make this lucky guy a father." He patted the Pigfoot on the shoulder.

The twins cried out, trying to get up. The scarred man held them firmly in place.

To Izzy's left, Redhead murmured under her breath, lips quivering.

"Don't be so scared," Clive said. "I've filmed decapitations, castrations, and several disembowelments but if there's one thing I've never had in my movies, it's rape. I despise those kinds of films. The world has enough horrible things in it already, so I've always steered clear of that stuff. I consider myself a humanitarian of sorts. But we do have to put some buns in those ovens so I'm going to leave it to my producer here—who also happens to oversee our effects department—to make that possible." He turned toward the naked woman. "Tara, time to work your magic."

The naked woman—Tara apparently—came to the front of the group. Again Izzy was fixated on her beauty. Her pale skin lacked imperfections, not a mole on its landscape or even a hint of cellulite. Her breasts fell perfectly on her chest, each the exact size as the other. Her eyes, though, were the most mesmerizing.

They were black. Totally, utterly black. No sign of whites or blood vessels, no irises to speak of. It was as if the pupils had dilated and devoured everything in their path.

She held a hand to the taller twin's face and hushed her. The sound was like a thousand snakes hissing, yet it was calming beyond description. Izzy's eyes grew heavy.

Tara took the other twin's chin into her hand. Both girls quieted. Both girls fixated on Tara's bone white face as she whispered something into Clive's ear. His smile widened and he signaled the Pigfoot to join their group.

"You seeing this shit?" CJ whispered.

"I'm seeing it," the scarred man said.

The Pigfoot put a hand—partly human, partly beast—onto Tara's shoulder and shut its eyes, fading into some sort of trance.

Izzy tried to look away but the power Tara held over them was too strong. Some force beyond her comprehension that wouldn't let her move a centimeter.

The scared and rational part of her screamed from within, told her to make her move. No one would notice. It was her last chance.

Then came a sound. Far away at first, something like rushing air, a tire being filled at a gas station. It grew closer. The twins fell onto their backs, convulsed, foaming at the mouth. Their eyes rolled back so that only the whites could be seen, the polar opposite of Tara's black orbs.

The flesh around their navels grew exponentially, skin stretching taut.

They're going to pop, Izzy thought, on the verge of hysteria. *Their stomachs are going to burst like failed balloon animals.*

And they did. Their stomachs tore open. Small forms clawed their way out of the twins' midsections. The things wiped away blood and innards and began to cry as they saw the world for the first time.

Part of Izzy, as sick as it seemed, was not surprised to see the two baby Pigfoots as they crawled out of the twins and stumbled toward their father. Or to witness the two once-blond girls, alive moments before, bleed out on the floor in front of her.

It was madness, a nightmare, a break with reality. Except all of it was real.

The redhead screamed. She elbowed the scarred man in the sternum and kicked CJ in the balls. Both men lost their balance before chasing after her.

Neither Clive nor Tara noticed, too amazed by the two new stars of their film.

"You think this batch will be different?" Clive said. "You think they'll follow orders better?"

The woman said nothing, only nodded in response.

This was it. Izzy's only chance at leaving this hell hole. She fled in the opposite direction as the redhead, past the cameras and out the front door. Instead of running toward the road or through the woods, she found the nearest bush and lay down, trying to silence her breathing as much as possible.

She waited for the sounds of footsteps. Surely CJ would come for her, his forked tongue wagging like a panting dog.

In the distance: a scream, undeniably female.

They'd caught the redhead.

"**J**ESUS, SLOW DOWN!" Liam held onto the door handle for support but it was no use. He flung from side to side in the passenger seat despite the seat belt locking into place.

"No way. We need to keep up." Michelle's eyes were narrowed slits and he hadn't seen her blink in the last ten minutes.

Up ahead the van with the Bone Saw logo swerved every few moments, like the driver was drunk out of his mind. Having met Clive, Liam wouldn't have been surprised. You'd need to be drunk to deal with a bastard like that every day.

Eventually the van turned onto a less-populated road, in a section of town housing more rednecks than tourists. After another mile it slowed and turned left, traveling a dirt path. Liam knew exactly where that road ended. If you followed it all the way, you'd wind up back in the town center, but along the way, you'd see a large Victorian mansion that looked ready to crumble. "Scary Harry," he said.

"What?" It was the first time she'd looked away from the windshield.

Liam nodded toward the path as they slowed. "A crazy guy lives up this way. They call him Scary Harry. His parents are rich or something. They bought him the house to keep him out of trouble."

"What kind of trouble?"

"The kind that involves screeching obscenities at the playground and pissing your pants in the supermarket."

"The house? Is it rundown?"

"From what I've heard. To tell you the truth I've never seen it myself. We used to tell ghost stories about the guy. How he lived in a haunted mansion and stole children from the beach. Chopped them up and made them into stews."

"Charming. Looks like you're going to see the place after all." She turned onto the path and cut the lights, keeping her distance. It seemed wrong for a shiny new Lexus to be out here in the woods.

"She's going to kill you," Liam said. "Jacqueline, I mean. You scratch this thing up and she's going to have a shit conniption."

"Let her. I can't believe you hang out with that bitch."

"It's not by choice. Corey is smitten with her. Don't ask me why but he is." He thought back to the way his friend had looked, furious as he held his thrashing girlfriend. Getting kicked in the balls hadn't helped matters much. But maybe if Corey was his *real* friend, he wouldn't have let his girlfriend speak to Liam that way in the first place. "I should thank you."

"For what?"

"For sticking up for me back there. She said a lot of nasty stuff. You didn't let her off the hook but you could have. You could've walked away."

"I guess I could have." She squeezed his thigh, sending fireworks throughout his body.

A few yards ahead the trees opened up to a large clearing. Scary Harry estate came into view. It was worse than he'd imagined. The peeling paint, rotten siding, and loose shingles made his skin run cold. "Can't we just go back to my apartment and finish getting drunk?"

"I'd love to but there are more important things going on."

He sighed as she pulled into the brush and cut the engine. Ahead, the van slowed and parked out front. Two men stepped out and jogged into the front door. For a moment light spilled from the entryway then the doors closed and everything lay covered in darkness again.

Liam tried to convince himself there wasn't anything hiding in the bushes. Nothing large and slimy would crawl from the shadows. The person or thing that had chased him the night before was not on its way toward the car, ready to finish the job. "Can I ask you a question?"

"Sure." She craned her neck, squinting at the upstairs windows. Wooden boards had been nailed over several and he didn't want to know why.

"But you have to answer honestly."

She nodded. "You know me."

No, I don't and that's the problem. "Why are we really out here? The way you looked at my poster of Clive, the way you reacted when you found out I'd met him . . . " He rubbed his jaw, still swollen and sore. "Not to mention the way you stole a car and chased after his van. There's something you're not telling me."

"You're right about that."

"So tell me."

She shook her head. "I'd rather not. Now's not a good time."

He sighed. "A guy came by yesterday morning looking for you. Said he needed to ask you a few questions."

Her eyes widened and she finally looked away from the mansion. "What kind of questions?"

"He wouldn't say but he seemed intent on finding you. I told him I didn't know what he was talking about."

"And he left?"

"Yes, but I have a feeling he'll be back."

She nibbled her bottom lip, teeth narrowly avoiding the piercing. Then she smiled. "That was probably the creep who chased me down last night. You did good." He wanted to kiss her, this mystery girl, but she was still hiding behind a lie.

So just come out with it then. He cleared his throat and studied her face. "Is your name Maura Black?"

She spun around. "What? What did you just say?"

"That guy. He said your name was Maura and I figured he was crazy, you know? He didn't seem all that sane to begin with. Must've had the wrong girl. But if you could see the way you look right now . . . "

She glared. He suddenly wanted to take his chances outside amid the dark trees. "Look, I'm sorry. You don't owe me any explanation. I ought to just head back and—"

"He's my father."

Liam paused. "Who is? The guy who was asking for you?"

"No. *He* is." She nodded toward the mansion.

He made the connection then, felt stupid for not making it sooner. The evidence had been in front of his eyes all along. "Clive? Clive is your . . . "

Her mouth curled into a snarl, nostrils flared like a bull. Tears stained her eyelids. "That's right. He's my father and I came to this shitty town to find him."

"I'm guessing it's not just to have a friendly chat."

"I plan on killing him."

"You can't be serious."

"Dead. If you only knew what a bastard that guy is. You think a black eye and bruised chin is bad? That's nothing compared to what he did to my mother and I."

Liam opened his mouth to ask her what she meant when he saw a shadow appear from the woods and move quickly toward the car.

It was a girl with tied up hands and tattered clothes.

She was covered head to toe with blood.

✷✷✷

The girl stopped in front of the car and studied Liam and Michelle through the windshield.

Maura, he reminded himself. *Her name is Maura Black and you've been smitten over someone who doesn't exist.*

The girl cocked her head, wobbling from side to side. She considered them for a long time before moving toward the driver's side window.

"We should go," Liam said. "We should put the car

in reverse and get the hell out of here now. This girl looks like she's lost her mind."

The closer she got, Liam saw it wasn't only blood that covered her skin. There were other things, unidentifiable chunks that could've been bone or bits of gore. He didn't want to think about how she'd come to be covered in them. "Mich—I mean Maura. Go. Now."

Maura shushed him. "Stop. She might be hurt."

"And it might be a trap. You said your father's a bad guy. I'm not going to argue with that. This might be a trick."

Maura rolled down the window.

The bloody girl stopped a few feet away. She looked back at the mansion and scanned her surroundings. "Are you with him?" Her voice quivered, her quick breaths not far from hyperventilating.

"Define 'him,'" Maura said.

"The movie guy. Clive Sherman. Are you part of his crew or something? Because if so, he let me walk away. This is . . . this is make-up. I'm getting ready for a shoot."

Liam could smell something rancid wafting off of her and something told him that wasn't corn syrup all over her skin.

"We're not with him," Maura said. "We're *against* him and his entire seedy operation. In fact, we came here to shut it down for good."

"*We* didn't come here for that," Liam mumbled. "One of us isn't that insane."

Maura elbowed him in the gut without looking away from the girl. "Will you bring us to him? Help us get in?"

The girl shook her head, looking childish now, a lost toddler who wanted her parents and teddy bear. "No. We need to get out of here as fast as possible. You don't know what's coming."

The front doors of the mansion slammed open, dim light flooding into the night. Shadows appeared in the entryway, one of them impossibly tall. They walked toward the Lexus.

"Those bastards." Maura gritted her teeth, fingers white-knuckled and clutched around the steering wheel. "I could take them all out right now. Hit the gas and hear them crunch under the wheels."

The girl wiped away tears and blood. "Please. You have to believe me. That place is hell."

The figures stepped closer. There were perhaps a half dozen. Most of them were tattooed men. Clive's crew, Liam supposed, but the tall one in the middle— it didn't look like a man at all.

Maura unlocked the doors. "Get in and buckle up."

The girl opened the back door and dove, huddled on the seat, saying they were fucked over and over like a mantra.

"Hold on," Maura said.

Before Liam could protest she turned the key, engine grumbling back to life. The headlights turned on, lighting up the darkness ahead. Lighting up the figures advancing.

Lighting up the tall, pinkish thing with a roid freak's body and a snout for a nose.

Liam's sanity threatened to fly away in the breeze. He was dreaming again. The thing would take off its mask and it would be Heather, taunting him, stabbing the knife deeper into his back. That had to be it.

Because the alternative meant that he was looking at the Pigfoot, not on a television screen and not on a VHS cover. In *real life*. The closer it got, the more he started to suspect the second theory. He was a fan boy after all, knew the creature better than anyone else.

It's a costume, you idiot. Clive's movies may be low-budget but he saves the bulk of the money for blood and guts. His special effects are rivaled by no one.

The Pigfoot grunted and spat something slimy onto the ground. There were no zippers of any kind along its dirt-covered body. It wasn't a guy in a costume, no matter how badly Liam wanted to believe it. It was real and it was coming to eat them.

Liam reached over and put the car in reverse.

"What're you doing?" Maura slapped his hand away. "We can run him over."

"It," the girl said from the backseat. "Not him. *It*."

The Pigfoot charged the car and jumped onto the hood, pink saliva dripping onto the window. The ooze steamed and wiggled like a pile of drenched worms. It brought two fists down onto the metal, leaving behind bowling ball-sized indentations.

I can already hear Jacqueline's tantrum, Liam thought hysterically. *I hear his stomach grumbling too. No. It. You heard the girl. It's not a man, it's a fucking monster.*

"You want revenge," he said. "That's fine. I get it. But back this car up now so we don't get fucking eaten!"

The Pigfoot wound back once more. The other figures were nearly at the car now. Among the crew were smaller figures he hadn't noticed before. Dog-sized shadows that, for a moment, looked like miniature version of the Pigfoot itself.

"Fuck." Maura floored the gas, the car spinning out for a moment. Liam said a few silent prayers, thought about his script at home, how it would never be finished.

The wheels evened out and the car spun backward. The Pigfoot lost its balance, falling and landing on two of the figures. Liam heard shouting, saw fingers pointing, and more of the figures gained on them.

Maura backed up until the lane opened wide enough to maneuver a three-point turn.

Liam tried not to look in the rearview mirror when they'd turned around. He wouldn't see his favorite monster come to life, he told himself. Surely there had to be a rational explanation.

When the path met the road he risked a glance.

And nearly pissed his pants when he saw a familiar shade of pink in the distance. It followed them for a half mile before they finally lost it.

The bloody girl began to laugh in between sobs. "I told you. Didn't I tell you?"

"WE LOST HER," CJ said as he stepped back inside Scary Harry's former home. He punched the doorframe and hissed through his teeth, bringing his knuckles to his mouth and sucking. "Someone in a Lexus came by and grabbed her."

"Could be worse." Clive was surprised how calm his own voice sounded. Under normal circumstances he'd would have been cursing and knocking equipment over. He'd broken more than a few cameras in his career. But now, in the aftermath—the after*birth*—he couldn't help but smile.

"What if she goes to the cops?" Tucker said. His scar gave him a sinister look but in reality he was a big baby. Clive had hired him as a grip but as with most low-budget films, he'd become a jack-of-all-trades. Except he sucked at most of them, complained every chance he got.

"Tucker, think for a minute," Clive said. "What

cop is going to believe her? She looks like Carrie on prom night and she's screaming about pig men."

Tucker seemed to consider this, absently itching his scar.

The three bodies lay on the floor, torn to shreds from the inside out. The redhead still twitched now and then, the nerves fighting even in death. Her breasts hung out of the shredded fabric of her shirt. It was a shame he hadn't filmed something with her prior to her death. She would've looked good coming out of the water, wearing not much or nothing at all. But the camera had captured something special tonight, something he ought to be proud of.

And it was all thanks to Tara. She was beautiful and terrifying at once. The crew always drooled in her company. They thought she was just a hot piece of ass with some sort of gift, a clairvoyant who also resembled a top-notch porn star. They didn't know the truth.

To be fair, neither did Clive.

He'd asked her time and again what she was, how she'd come to resemble in such exact detail a fictional character he'd invented. She never gave him a straight answer. He'd thought about it for countless hours, supposed she could've been a siren or a vampire or a she-demon but whatever she was he'd offered himself to her in exchange for his life.

He remembered that day of location scouting gone wrong, feeling reborn, a second chance at living. He'd prepared himself for the worst after he agreed to her deal, expected this nude beauty to reach out with a claw and drag him straight to Hades. But she'd been more creative than that. All she required were a few sacrifices.

A few meaning an entire town's worth.

"So what the hell happens next?" CJ said, still scanning the perimeter of the yard, as if Izzy was going to run back and hop into his arms. His forked tongue drooped out of his mouth like a sad puppy.

"We pack up," Clive said. "There are still some hours left tonight and we need to get filming before the sun comes up."

"You know, it would help if we had a script. We could—and call me crazy here—actually plan these things out." CJ had balls. Clive would give him that much. Few people were brave enough to mouth off to him.

"You're a cameraman on a micro-budget horror movie. All you've got to do is point the lens toward the blood and shoot it. And that's the plan. Isn't that right, Tara?"

"Yes." Her voice, once harsh and eerie, was now angelic to his ears. She signaled him, curling her index finger. His skin tingled and the fabric near his crotch tightened. When their faces were inches away, she touched a smooth hand to the back of his neck and brought their foreheads together.

This was where CJ had been wrong. There *was* a script, only it wasn't written in ink and it didn't exist in this world. It lay in some dark place, in Tara's mind if she had one. She was the true director here. And the producer, screenwriter, and set designer.

Clive fell into a trance, his feet falling from under him. Weightless, a balloon on a windy day. He floated above the shithole that was Bass Falls, saw countless roofs of summer homes, sandy beaches, and the wide expanse of the Atlantic Ocean, which seemed to stretch forever. He knew the film's finale was coming up. In this astral projection, glimpse of the future, or whatever this truly was, he could hear screams in the distance, fires crackling, alarms sounding. He smelled a million different scents, all equally pleasing to his nostrils: fire and blood and salt water.

His astral self dove to the ground, no longer soaring like a plane. It flew toward the city center, past the shops and cafes, landing on an unassuming brick building that reminded him of a hospital.

"No, not a hospital," Tara said inside his mind, riding a subway system of neurons. "Even better."

"The police station," Clive said, the answer dawning on him. He couldn't be sure if he'd spoken the words in this trance or the real world, perhaps both.

"Yes," Tara said. "They'll be helpless."

Of course. It made perfect sense. A small town like this, they couldn't have more than twenty cops on their force. Wipe most of them out and you lessened the chances that their final act would be meddled with.

"I love you," Clive told Tara, not for the first time. And he meant it. It wasn't a hollow statement like it had been with Lisa. She'd been fine for a while but time had sagged her skin and hardened her mood. She'd turned into a nagging husk of his former lover. And he couldn't forget about his daughter—though he would've liked to. She was weak, perhaps more so than her mother. They didn't appreciate him, didn't understand him anywhere close to the way Tara did.

"I own you," she said, as if he needed a reminder.

"Yes. You do. And I wouldn't have it any other way."

He fell farther to the ground, the visions breaking

just before he hit the concrete. Then he was back in the hermit's mansion. *Clive's* mansion now. What remained of Scary Harry's body lay in the basement, rotting and decaying. Food for spiders.

His crew eyed him like he was mad. He wasn't sure what he looked like when he went into Tara's trances but from their expressions he assumed it was less than ordinary.

The Pigfoot had led his three new offspring to the mess on the floor. They lapped at the blood and intestines like hungry kittens, moaning with enjoyment. Their first meal. A moment to be remembered. Piggy was going to be a good father.

"Let's load up. We're going to cast some cops for this next scene."

CJ and Tucker beamed.

Roger, their driver and grip and occasional murderer, stepped into the living room from the kitchen, sipping a beer and holding a half-eaten sandwich. He was the only one who never seemed fazed by any of this madness. To Roger this was just a gig no matter how much blood and death it entailed. "I'll pull the van around back." He ran outside like a child on Christmas morning.

Tara took Clive's hand and together they got ready to film their best scene yet.

OFFICER PETE FARMER struggled with old man Bruce as he brought him through the front doors of the Bass Falls police station and into the holding area. The guy's full name was Kenny Richards and Peter hadn't the slightest idea where the Bruce moniker had originated. He didn't know a whole lot about Bruce except that he was one of many town drunks and he smelled like a combination of piss and shit with a bit of vomit thrown in for good measure.

"I'm telling you, he's dead," Bruce said as Pete escorted him to one of three holding cells. He was a frequent visitor. So much so that they'd come to call the first cell on the left Bruce's quarters. Pete opened the door, tossed the bum in, and quickly locked it again.

Bruce regained his balance and slammed rotten hands against the bars. "Are you even listening to a word I'm saying?" His breath was a cloud of cheap whiskey and cigarettes.

Pete brought his arm to his nose and mouth, speaking through the vacuum lock. "I've listened to all of it and I'd like you to give it a rest. You sound even crazier than usual. And that's saying something."

"I ain't crazy," Bruce said, though Pete and just about every resident of Bass Falls begged to differ. "I saw him for sure. He was buried up to his neck in the sand. His head was a mess. Looked like someone put his face in a vice grip and didn't let go until they pulped him good."

"I'm sure." Pete returned his cuffs to his belt compartment. "Listen, you have yourself a good nap and things will look better in the morning."

Bruce slapped the bars one last time before keeling over. "Son, I know I ain't nothing much compared to you. I sleep on the beach when it's warm and I live on day-old hot dogs. You got no reason to believe me but I'm asking you this one time. Marty Randall was my friend and he didn't deserve nothing like that. Just go check it out and you'll see for yourself."

Pete sighed and rubbed his temples, hoping to hold off the oncoming headache. He couldn't help but feel for the old man. He had no family that Pete knew of, no home, no future. "I'll tell you what. You settle down and don't say another word, I'll have someone check it out later."

Bruce sniffled, wiped snot from his nose, and nodded. "Thank you, Officer. I mean it."

"Goodnight, Bruce." Pete headed for the doors, stopping by the desk on his way out. Glenn, the night watchman, had nodded off, the brim of his hat pushed over his eyes.

Pete slapped him across the back of his head.

Glenn shot up, looking around like he expected to see a robbery in progress. It took him a moment to register Pete's laughter. "You bastard."

"I couldn't resist." He lowered his voice. "If that old man starts losing his shit, come get me. He's even more off his rocker tonight. Said his friend got his head squashed or something. Made me promise him I'd go check it out."

Glenn rolled his eyes, still catching his breath. "Have fun with that."

Pete laughed. "I'll have fun sitting my ass down and waiting out the rest of my shift."

"You're not going to check it out?"

"What do you think? You believe a word that guy says?"

They watched for a moment as Bruce blew chunks into his toilet.

"You make a good point."

Pete patted him on the back. "You have yourself a good night and try staying awake for a change."

Pete stepped through the double doors toward the cubicles. He sat down at his desk and thought about filing a report for Bruce but decided it could wait until tomorrow. Truth be told, he didn't hate the paperwork like most cops. Sure, he was shocked at how boring the job was when he'd started two years prior but he hadn't expected it to be the LAPD either. Bass Falls was a sleepy town and nothing much happened here. Unless you asked Bruce.

He looked at the picture of his wife, the frame sitting on his desk beside his *World's Best Dad* mug, given to him by his daughter Kelly. He and Sheila had tried to conceive the first six years of their marriage. The doctors had told him he was shooting blanks.

They ought to consider adoption. But one morning he'd woken to Sheila holding a pregnancy test. Beaming. Even doctors were wrong sometimes.

He thought about calling her now, asking how Kelly was sleeping, but he didn't want to wake her if she'd nodded off herself. She was grumpy when she was tired, which was about the only complaint he had. He'd lucked out in the marriage department and he never let himself take his wife for granted.

He sat back in his chair, yawning and stretching. Eight minutes before his shift ended. Martinez and Holt would be arriving anytime now. Landers and Stairwell were in the break room, laughing at something near the coffee machine. It was the most work he'd seen them do all day.

He leaned farther back, eyes growing heavy. Maybe he'd just take a nap for the remainder of his shift.

From the back hall, voices shouted.

He caught eyes with Landers and Stairwell just as the lights went out.

Landers let out a yelp that didn't match his hulk of a body. He was well over six feet, could bench his own body weight, but he sounded like a little girl.

Pete fumbled through his desk for a flashlight. He knocked over his mug with the back of his hand. It rolled onto the floor and porcelain cracked. He opened the bottom right drawer and found the light, flipping on the switch and looking at his Father's Day present, which now lay in three separate sections. Part of him wanted to mourn the loss but that part hushed when the noises from the back hall grew louder.

He shined the light toward the break room,

illuminating Landers and Stairwell. Both had their guns drawn, hands shaking badly. They'd each been on the force for nearly a decade and Pete had to wonder how often they'd used their firearms. Judging by their posture it wasn't often enough.

Pete took out his own gun, criss-crossing it over the arm with the flashlight as he'd been trained. He shined the light at the door and listened.

Scream. Shouts. Growls.

He caught eyes with the other officers, hoping they heard the same things, hoping he wasn't losing his mind like Bruce. Their faces were all the confirmation he needed.

The door bulged. Something large struck the other side. He hoped Glenn was okay.

Of course he is. You just patted him on the back five minutes ago. Nothing major could've happened in that short of a time. There's a perfectly good explanation for this.

He took two nervous steps toward the door and froze when the knob turned. It took an eternity to open, rusty hinges groaning like someone on their deathbed.

A figure appeared in the doorway. It stumbled forward, limping badly.

Pete shined the light and saw that it was Glenn. Emphasis on the *was*. Because Glenn was torn apart. There were slashes along his face and neck, dripping fountains of blood that pooled beneath him. One arm lay at a crooked angle, bone jutting out like a knife and the other was gone altogether. His feet hovered a few inches above the floor. It took a moment for Pete to realize that someone was holding him up.

From behind his body came another grunt, much

louder this time, much less human. Whatever it was breathed deeply and was large enough to lift a dead man without effort.

His instincts shouted at him for perhaps the first time since joining the force. Whatever was back there was too much for the three of them to handle. Holt and Martinez were due any second but Pete couldn't count on their intervention. For the moment they were alone and they needed to fall back.

He turned to tell the other two officers to retreat but Stairwell already had his gun raised and clicked off two quick rounds into Glenn's dead face. Glenn's right eye came apart.

"Hold your fire!" Pete said but his words were lost as the grunts sounded again.

More of them now. Multiple figures back there, making their way into the office. Glenn's body shook, seizure-like, and was thrown forward, travelling over several cubes and knocking over the computer to Pete's right.

Now that the doorway was clear he saw largest of the intruders.

When Pete was in college he'd dated a girl who loved horror movies. She got off on the gory parts, used to blow him whenever someone got torn apart. Those kinds of films were trash but he wasn't complaining either. He'd gone along with it for a couple years until she died of an overdose. It was his knowledge of those films that helped him identify the thing in front of him.

It was the Pigfoot.

Not some costume or cardboard cutout but the *real deal*, like it had stepped out of a dingy VHS box and into the Bass Falls police department.

And it had company.

Three miniature versions leapt through the doorway and charged the break room. Stairwell shot off another thirteen rounds until his clip was empty. One of the pigs dove onto his face and ripped off his nose in a single chomp.

Landers backed away, dropped his gun, continued screaming. He held up his hands like a shield. The closest pig dug in, ripping all ten digits, bone and all, away from the knuckles. Landers stopped screaming after that.

From the hall Bruce howled, not out of lunacy but pain. There were other shapes back there. Human shapes. In fact Pete thought he saw lights and a microphone, maybe even a camera.

Bruce was fucking right. There was *a murder and there were just four more. Get the hell out of here and call for backup.*

Pete spun around, opened the door, and fled into the front area of the station.

He was met with another cameraman. The guy held his foot out and tripped Pete, sending him face-first onto the floor and chipping a few teeth in the process. He tried to get back up but the guy held him down with his foot, calling for someone named Clive to get their ass over here and start directing.

Pete managed to lift his head and saw three unmoving bodies a few feet away. Holt and Martinez had shown up, after all, but they hadn't made it very far. Both their heads had been caved in, bits of skull scattered around their faces. The third belonged to Maria Sadler, the dispatcher. Her head was fully in tact but both her eyes had been removed, two empty caverns left in their wake.

Pete's hands were empty. Where was his gun? He couldn't remember if he'd dropped it on the way. Rookie mistake. He should've gone to the LAPD, after all. At least he would've been more prepared for emergencies. He wished he'd left early tonight or that he'd gone to check on Bruce's dead friend.

Most of all he wished his *World's Best Dad* mug hadn't broken.

He moved his head upward and bit into the camera guy's calf. Warm, coppery blood flooded his mouth. The guy swore and stepped off and Pete stood, catching his balance. So close. He could smell the ocean, hear his daughter laughing.

Someone grabbed his shoulders, tossed him against the wall. His vision blurred. His head swelled, a concussion, though it was the least of his worries.

The Pigfoot and his little friends, as in-fucking-sane as it seemed, charged toward him, snouts sniffing, mouths leaking an assortment of bodily fluids.

The rest of the crew followed and Pete heard one of them say they had a great shot.

Then he heard nothing else.

"**I**T'S DEAD," Liam said, the phone against his ear.

"What do you mean 'it's dead?'" Maura sipped a beer, a cigarette dangling out of her mouth. A bit of ash fell to the floor, joining the rest of the mess from the party earlier that night.

"I mean there's no busy signal or anything. It's just dead. I'll try again." He hung up and started dialing once more but Maura grabbed his arm.

"You've tried enough. Plus I don't want any cops coming over here."

He ripped away from her clutch and continued dialing. "We *need* to call them, all things considered." They both looked at the girl on the bed, Izzy as they'd come to learn, though that was about as much information as she was willing to offer. Liam had insisted they take her to the hospital but Izzy wasn't having it. Something about her parents finding out. Great, he'd thought. Another runaway. They'd at least convinced her to shower when they got back to Liam's apartment. She'd spent a half hour under scolding water. Her skin was pink now. Liam wasn't sure if it was from the heat or if the blood was just stubborn.

"We can just drop her off at the station," Maura said, a cloud of mist spilling from her mouth. It was the first time he'd seen her smoke, which was somewhat of a turn-off. Then again she wasn't the girl he'd been drooling over, was she? Michelle had turned out to be a fantasy and nothing more.

"I'm not setting foot outside after what we saw tonight," Liam said, still holding the phone above him like a brother stealing a toy from his sister. "That *thing* is out there."

Maura rolled her eyes. "Don't start that shit again. It was a guy in a costume. A particularly convincing costume but a costume just the same. You were scared and it was dark but it wasn't the monster from my dad's movies."

"That's where you're wrong. I've seen that thing a thousand times. I know it like the back of my hand. There were no zippers, no seams. It was real and before you give me a hard time, no, I don't have any theories as to how that's possible. I'm just telling you what I saw."

"What you *thought* you saw."

He waved her off. This was going nowhere. He dialed the police station two more times, both unsuccessful. "Son of a bitch." He tossed his phone across the room. It landed behind the TV and he heard the undeniable sound of cracking plastic. On the television screen, *The Evil Dead* was suspended in time.

Izzy rocked back and forth on the couch, a blanket

wrapped around her like a robe. She mumbled something too softly for his ears to pick up. The only other information they'd been able to pry was that she'd been tricked into being in Clive's movie.

Maura touched Liam's shoulder. He flinched. "Jesus, don't sneak up on me like that."

"You need to calm down. They didn't get a good look at us and even if they did, they haven't got your address. No one's going to come barging in here tonight."

He looked at the door in the kitchen, all its locks fastened, and tried to tell himself he agreed with her. "What the hell was your plan anyway?"

Maura finished her beer and tossed the cigarette butt into the can. "How do you mean?"

"Your plan. Your endgame. Why did you come to Bass Falls? Did you think you were going to scare Clive? Or were you honestly planning on killing him?"

"That's none of your business."

He reminded her of the mumbling girl on his sofa, not to mention the scratched up Lexus parked out front. "I'd say it's been made my business, wouldn't you?"

Maura did her best to look tough before finally sighing. "Look, I didn't mean for you to get mixed up with this. I noticed you were wearing that stupid *Blonde Bimbo Holocaust* shirt at the coffee shop."

"*Massacre.*"

"Whatever. I figured maybe you knew about my dad's movie. Then when I found out you'd met him, I had to keep you close. You were my lead."

"Glad I could help." He gritted his teeth and wished she would transform back into Michelle, back into the girl he'd thought she was.

"I'm sorry if I led you on. I really am. But you don't understand how despicable that man is."

"I know what it's like to not get along with your parents, Maura. Mine aren't exactly angels either. I haven't talked to them in months. They gave up on me the moment I dropped out of school, just cut me out like I didn't exist. When people ask them about me, they either shrug or change the subject. My aunt's no better. The longest conversations we have are about whether or not I can pay my rent on time this month."

She started to laugh, just a chuckle at first but it quickly grew to full-on giggles.

"What the hell's so funny?"

She wiped away tears, shook her head, and her face turned to a sneer. "I'm sorry. It must be tough on you, what with your parents being mad and living in the same town and never raising a hand to you. Tell me, did you ever hide under your bed when your dad came home? Do you know what it's like to hear your mother get beaten night after night? I didn't happen to see any bruises and scars on you so I'd say you're overreacting."

"I took a good look at you last night too and everything seemed to check out okay."

"Look again." She came toward him so that their faces were inches away and pulled up her sleeve, revealing her tattoo. A flower of some sort, perhaps an orchid. It was hard to make out. Liam had initially blamed it on a bad artist but now, this close, he saw the flesh beneath the ink was distorted. "That's from an iron," she said.

"A what?"

She nodded. "That's right. My mother was ironing one day and Clive was sipping on his whiskey and writing one of his shitty scripts at the dinner table. I was playing with my doll and I tripped. I was a clumsy kid. My mom used to call me Maura the Destroyer because I left a wake of destruction in my path. I knocked over my dad's drink all over his script. You know the funniest part, the real kicker of it all? He didn't even need to do it because he had a digital copy. He stood up, smacked me across the face, grabbed the iron." She paused, looking at Liam like he'd morphed into Clive. "He held me down. My mom tried to help but he kicked her legs out from underneath. He smiled at me, that tacky little pirate tooth twinkled, and he brought the iron down."

She touched the orchid softly. "I swear it still hurts to this day. Probably more in my head than anything else."

His throat was dry, his voice just above a whisper. "I'm sorry. I didn't know."

She shook her head. "No, you didn't. But now you do and now you've got to promise me you'll help me get him. I'm not the only one he's hurt." She pointed to Izzy. "That girl has no cuts of her own from what I can see and if you remember correctly, she was covered head to toe in blood."

Liam hadn't thought of that. If the Pigfoot was real—and he was sure of it despite what Maura said— then it wasn't hard to believe the blood had been real too. He thought of Clive, that bastard, as he held poor Maura down and burned her flesh. He thought of innocent people getting hurt in the name of his low-budget films. He touched his jaw, the bruised skin still sensitive. "Okay. I'll help you."

"You mean it?"

He nodded. "I promise. Whatever you need."

She held a hand out. "Shake on it."

He bypassed it, drew her close, and kissed her.

His mind screamed at him.

What the hell are you doing, Romeo? She isn't Michelle. She isn't the girl you thought you were falling for. She isn't even Heather. At least she used to kiss you out of pity. This girl is tough as nails and she wants nothing more than friendship. She wanted to shake your goddamned hand, not French you.

Yet she didn't pull away. If anything she pulled him closer. Touched the back of his neck, massaging the skin. She lifted a leg, rubbing her knee against him. Her kisses turned more desperate, like she needed him. He almost smiled but stopped short for fear it would ruin the mood. It felt good to be needed by someone, to not live in constant rejection like he wasn't any better than a pile of garbage.

She mumbled something mid-kiss.

He pulled away, trying to catch his breath. "Sorry. I didn't mean to be forward. I should've asked."

She kissed his cheek. "Don't be stupid. I asked if you had somewhere else more . . . private." She nodded toward the futon.

Liam had forgotten about Izzy. The girl had stopped rocking and was looking everywhere but into the kitchen. Her cheeks were flushed and something like a guilty smile crossed her face. It was the first time she'd resembled a human all night.

"Bedroom." Liam nodded toward the second door in the kitchen. "There's a bedroom."

Maura smiled, grabbed his hand, and pulled him along. He tried not to look at Izzy on the way. He was willing to bet his cheeks were just as red as hers.

The bedroom was more of a storage unit for

horror movies, toys, and posters. In the corner lay a futon, its mattress even more ancient and worn as the couch in the living room, which was why he rarely slept in here.

"Is this where you keep all your torture porn?" Maura kicked off her shoes and unclasped her belt.

"Maybe." He tried to sound adventurous but inside he was melting. *This is really happening. You're about to sleep with a goddess.*

It was a short ordeal, just shy five minutes, but it was better than anything he'd ever had with Heather. When it was over, Maura leaned forward and kissed him.

He turned to see her laughing at him.

"Was it that bad?" he said.

"No, it was fine. It was great. You're just funny, that's all."

She kissed him once more then turned around, pulling his arm over her. She fell asleep moments later and he wasn't too far behind.

He smiled while he dreamed Heather-free dreams for the first time in a long time.

✳✳✳

Maura waited until Liam was asleep before she gently removed his hand from her shoulder and stood up to dress. She had several false starts, hating herself for what she was about to do, but in the end she chose to leave.

It wasn't that she didn't trust Liam. He'd promised to help her and she believed him. The problem was that he'd grown infatuated and the feeling was becoming mutual. She watched him sleeping, a smile on his face while he snored softly. A

145

tiny string of drool plopped off his lips and onto the floor. She forced back a giggle.

He was a good guy and *that* was the problem.

If she asked him to spin around five times and run headfirst into the nearest wall he would've done it without question. She wasn't his bitchy ex-girlfriend. She didn't get off on holding power over him. And she couldn't put him in any more danger.

So that's it, then? You're just going to fuck and duck out? How's that any better than his she-devil ex?

No, it wasn't like that. She'd wanted to be with him tonight. But there were bigger issues at hand.

Now that she knew where her father was staying, she'd go there alone and finish this once and for all.

She opened the door, wincing as it creaked, and took one last look at Liam, wishing they could have met under different circumstances, then stepped into the kitchen.

Izzy had fallen asleep sitting up. She snored loudly, mumbling every so often about baby pigs eating their mothers. It sounded like one hell of nightmare.

Before leaving, Maura paid a visit to the kitchen counter. She looked through the drawers until she found the largest of the knives. It was a chef's model that had seen better days, something likely purchased on QVC eons ago. The blade was rusty and faded but it looked sharp enough. She ran her thumb along the edge and winced as a tiny incision opened along her flesh. A bead of blood seeped out and she licked it clean.

She tore off a few paper towels, wrapped the blade, and slipped it into the band of her jeans, pulling her shirt over the handle.

On her way out she noticed the poster of Clive had been taken down. She didn't believe in fate, thought you had to make your own way in life, but she took that as a good omen just the same.

She closed the door quietly behind her, descended the stairs, and stepped into the night. Her skin went rigid against the temperature. It had been muggy earlier but the air had since grown chilly. She was still sweaty from sleeping with Liam. She smiled again, thinking of him beneath her, innocent in some strange way but also more of a man than any of her prior boyfriends.

She thought that maybe if this all played out well, if what she was about to do wasn't traced back to her, she just might pay him another visit. She could picture herself sleeping next to him, watching horror movies—none from Bone Saw Studios of course—and drinking too much cheap beer. The vision sent pleasant squirms throughout her belly.

Jacqueline's car was parked along the curb, covered in scratches, the paint scraped away to reveal the metal underneath in several places. That bitch was going to have a meltdown when she found out. Maura was glad she'd be missing the spectacle.

She considered running back upstairs to grab the keys but decided against it. She couldn't just pull up to the house this time. It was a long walk but at least she'd have the element of surprise on her side.

She started down Liam's street, rubbing her arms against the breeze, when she heard tapping behind her. She stopped and cocked her head. The noise ceased. She was being paranoid.

Until it started up again.

Footsteps. Just behind her, like an echo of her

own footfalls. She sped up. The other set of feet did the same, except faster.

She broke into a run, dreadlocks flowing in the wind like snakes. The paper towels itched the skin of her stomach and she imagined them tearing, revealing the blade beneath and sinking into the flesh. But she couldn't stop or her pursuer would gain on her.

It was one of Clive's crewmembers. It had to be. They'd followed her to Liam's place. Hell, it was probably the guy wearing the Pigfoot costume. She'd been so stupid to underestimate her father. Even if he hadn't seen that it was her in the car when they'd made their escape, he'd still make sure there were no witnesses.

At the corner of the street, she spun around, thinking she could surprise the guy, maybe knock him on his ass and head back the way she'd come.

But he was too fast. Approaching quickly, he grabbed onto her shoulders and pushed her down. She rolled over twice and tried to crawl away.

The guy dragged her toward him by her ankles, concrete searing her elbows, and flipped her over so that she could see his mangy face and dark eyes.

She recognized him right away as the man who had chased after her the night before, the same guy who'd no doubt questioned Liam. At the time she'd thought he was just a creep but now she knew he was connected to Clive. "Do you work for him, you asshole?" She tried to kick away his hands but failed.

"No. Now stop struggling."

"I don't believe you. I'll scream."

"Go ahead." He looked ready to topple over, riding high on something or perhaps coming down.

"Let go of me and I won't kill you." She tried to sound tough but her voice quivered.

"Give me a break." He kneeled on her chest, pinning her to the sidewalk. "Look, I'm not going to hurt you. Your mother hired me."

"Hired you for what?"

He clasped her wrists. "To find you before you do something stupid. I'd say it's too late for that but things could be a lot worse. I'm going to bring you back and she's going to pay me a lot of money. And you're not going to give me a hard time. Sound good?"

She spit in his face.

He sighed, showed his teeth, and wiped his cheek.

"What are you, some sort of private dick?"

He didn't answer.

"Yeah, you're a dick all right. I thought those only existed in bad movies."

"Shut up."

"Make me."

He turned his head suddenly and started talking to someone but when she followed his line of sight there was only a bush and crushed juice box on the ground. "I'm fine. This is it. I bring her back and I'm done. I'll get another job, one where I'm not so stressed." He groaned and shook his head at nothing. "Listen to you. I don't have high blood pressure. I get it checked twice a year. Yes, my cholesterol is fine. Better than fine actually. No, *you* listen. I'm not sick and you're not real."

He loosened his grip slightly while he talked to his imaginary friend. She pushed him away, stood up, and kicked him as hard as she could in the balls. That was twice in one night. It was becoming her signature move. He cupped his crotch, grew blue in the face, and keeled over.

She started to run again, was going to find Clive and make him pay. Her orchid seemed to emanate heat as if agreeing with her.

Something tripped her.

She fell for the second time and saw the man standing above her, one hand still holding his genitals. Blood dripped down her skinned elbow, staining her shirt and shorts. "Sorry about that," he said, trying to catch his breath. "And this." He wound back and slapped her across the face.

The world turned white then black.

LIAM WOKE AND forgot for a moment where he was. He hadn't slept in the storage room—the actual bedroom—in months. Everything that had happened in the last few days came back to him and he couldn't help but smile. Despite his bruised chin and almost getting killed and the realization that his favorite movie monster was somehow real, he was happy. Happier then he'd been in the last year or maybe longer.

He rubbed his eyes and wondered if he should turn around. He'd been spooning Maura when he fell asleep but he'd rolled over at some point during the night. Maybe he could kiss her until she woke. His morning erection throbbed in agreement. Perhaps they could go for round two.

Don't push your luck. Maybe she had a few too many of your beers and made a poor decision. She's probably staring at the ceiling and rolling her eyes this very moment, wondering why the hell she slept with you.

He shook his head, quieting the thoughts. For once, he decided, he was going to let himself be happy. For once he was going to take his life into his own hands.

He turned over, ready to touch her shoulder, but caressed the damp mattress instead.

His erection shriveled. She was probably in the kitchen, trying to get more information from Izzy and cooking some breakfast. There were plenty of eggs and bacon in the fridge. Breakfast was his favorite meal of the day. Not to mention the cheapest.

He sniffed the air and smelled nothing but dust from the unmoved boxes of memorabilia surrounding him.

In the living room, the television was still paused, the demonic tree branch frozen. Izzy slept on the couch at an awkward angle, her arms and head dangling off the edge.

He looked for a note, thinking she must have just stepped out and would be right back and also thinking how stupid and naïve he was. She'd ducked out on him, just as he'd feared she would. She was no better than Heather after all.

She's not the problem here. With all the presented evidence, you, sir, are quite leaveable.

He stopped pacing and wondered if she'd gotten into some sort of trouble. Was she dumb enough to go back to Scary Harry's mansion? No, not dumb but certainly crazy enough. He grabbed his phone from behind the television and dialed her number. Just as he'd feared, the screen was cracked, everything distorted. It rang only once before going to voicemail. Which meant she'd deliberately shut it off. Which meant she didn't want to talk to him.

He called again and left a message just the same, asking her to contact him the moment she got his voicemail.

The house became too humid, too closed in for his comfort. He needed to leave.

He grabbed Jacqueline's keys and heard a rustling sound from the living room.

Izzy had woken. She sat up, stretching and yawning. "Coffee?" Her throat was hoarse and her hair was wild.

He pointed. "In the cupboard. Listen, I need to do something real quick. Do you think you'll be okay here for a little while? You can help yourself to anything in the kitchen."

She nodded. "Sure. I do okay on my own. Are you positive you don't mind leaving a stranger in your apartment?"

He shrugged. "Unless you like horror movies, there isn't much to steal."

She looked around at the posters and countless movies. "You've got a point. Lucky for you I'm more of an action fan."

He forced a smile. "Great. I'll be back soon and we can talk about . . . last night."

"You mean Clive Sherman and the Pigfoot?"

He swallowed, thinking how crazy and accurate she sounded. "Yes. About that."

"I'll be here."

He turned around to leave.

"Oh and Liam?"

He stopped, the door halfway open. "Yeah?"

"She left last night. Or this morning. It was either really late or really early."

He sighed, trying to hide his anger.

"But she didn't seem like she was in a hurry. I pretended to be asleep. She looked . . . happy. You got yourself a good girlfriend."

"She's not my girlfriend." He thanked her and ran downstairs, wincing as he saw Jacqueline's car in the morning sunlight.

It looked a thousand times worse than the night before.

$$***$$

Twenty minutes later he parked the Lexus along the curb outside Jacqueline's house. It was a mile away from his aunt's home and was roughly three times as large. Her father was a surgeon of some sort in Boston and he spoiled his daughter like she was a celebrity. Liam had only set foot inside the place once and his jaw had hung open the entire time.

Now, though, his jaw hung open for a different reason. He cut the engine and peered toward every window of the house facing the street. He didn't see Jacqueline in any of them but he still felt watched, like she'd storm out the front door at any moment, ready to claw his eyes out.

The worst part was that he couldn't blame her. As much as he despised Jacqueline he was the one in the wrong. He'd gone off with a girl he didn't know and now the car looked like it had survived a grizzly attack. There were two large indentations on the hood, the spot where the Pigfoot had landed. Not to mention the blood stains in the backseat from Izzy. It resembled a fresh murder scene.

And how do you expect to pay for it?

He remembered the crumpled check in his pocket. It was only one hundred dollars but it was something.

Then again, reading the scribbled name on the check, he wasn't so sure he wanted the money that badly.

He stepped up to the front door, took a deep breath, and slid the keys through the mail slot.

Then he ran as if chased by the Pigfoot.

★★★

He called her a dozen more times, getting her voicemail after just one ring. She was ignoring him and he couldn't help but worry. But why should he? She'd lied to him, put him and his friends in danger.

And she slept with you—slept next *to you. Face it, you're a lonely bastard. She made you feel like a human being again.*

He needed to talk to someone, needed to get his mind off things.

He walked to Corey's apartment and knocked on the door. A cloud of smoke drifted out and reggae music assaulted Liam's ears.

"You got a second to talk?" Liam said, coughing into his hand.

Corey rolled his eyes and waved him inside.

The apartment smelled like weed and mildew but it was still cleaner than Liam's place. There were baggies of pot everywhere you looked. Corey had started out selling as a side job but he was almost full time now. He'd gone to college for two years, graduated with honors, and was now a professional drug dealer.

And he was doing a whole lot more with his life than Liam.

Corey sat in a recliner and muted the stereo and TV. On the screen, a mustached man was advertising the sharpest knife set in the world. He sliced silently into a pork chop and Liam forced back a shiver.

"You've got balls coming here," Corey said.

Liam winced. "I take it she saw the car?"

He nodded, puffed, coughed. "Just got off the phone with her after an hour. She said she's going to castrate you."

"Can't say I blame her. Listen. Tell her not to worry. I'll pay for it, no matter how much it comes to."

Corey snorted, said something under his breath.

"What was that?"

"I said with what money?"

"Look, you don't have to be an asshole about it. I said I'd figure it out and I will."

Corey finished the joint and set the roach onto the coffee table for future use. It joined several others. "How long have we been friends?"

"Is that rhetorical?"

Corey ignored him. "Going on fifteen years now. I know you better than anyone, better than your own parents. And I also know that you're not going to pay her back. It doesn't matter how many times you say you will. It doesn't even matter if *you* believe *yourself*. I'll end up forking over the money, even though her dad's a rich douche bag, and you'll promise to pay me back. But let's cut the shit, okay? I'm not holding my breath for that day to come."

Liam coughed again, waving away the smoke. Usually the smell of Corey's place was pleasant. You could get a nice buzz going if you stayed long enough. But today it smelled toxic, made his eyes water and his skin itch. "Why are you being such a dick? I came by to talk and you're giving me a guilt trip? You wouldn't believe the night I had."

"That's just it," Corey said. "I do believe it. Because every night—and day for that matter—is so terrible and awful for you. I get that you went through a rough patch. Heather dumped your ass and it took its toll on you but when's it going to end? When are you going to stop moping around and actually do something for a change?"

"This isn't about Heather."

"Buddy, you won't be saying that for a long time. Even with your new girl. Not if you keep this pathetic streak going. Don't take this the wrong way, but you're kind of a loser."

Liam's eyes watered and he suspected it wasn't from the smoke.

I will not cry in front of my best friend, no matter how much of a bastard he's being. I'm a grown man.

Was he? Grown men had jobs and lives and didn't spend their time in their aunt's in-law apartment. They didn't drop out of school because they were heartbroken. They didn't sit around all day watching horror movies.

The infomercial was still going. The crowd cheered on mute as the mustached man sliced deeper into a pork roast. Fresh blood seeped onto the cutting board.

"You okay, man?"

Liam shook his head. "What?"

"Look, I didn't mean to dig into you like that but I think you needed to hear it from me."

Liam gritted his teeth. "Yeah, maybe so. But you could've been nicer."

"Says the guy who trashed my girlfriend's car."

"Fuck your girlfriend."

Corey stood from the recliner. "Come again?"

Liam nodded, his heart pounding, just as shocked as Corey at what he'd said. "That's right. Fuck her. She's playing you and you know it. The only reason you stick around is because she's got you wrapped around her pretty little fake-tanned fingers. I may not be an expert in the girl department but I know trouble when I see it. Maura was right. You're going to realize it sooner or later."

For the second time in as many days, Liam saw his best friend grow angry. It seemed foreign, like he'd put on a Halloween mask. "Who the hell is Maura? I thought her name was Michelle. And where do you get off talking to me like that?"

"So you can comment on my shitty life but I can't say a thing about yours?"

Corey pointed to the door. "Ten seconds. I'm giving you ten seconds to get the hell out of here and not come back. That's because of those fifteen years I mentioned. Consider it a favor. Anyone else and I would've tossed them out already."

Liam's chin throbbed, as if reminding him that he'd already been hurt enough in recent times. Without saying anything else, he turned around, stepped outside, and slammed the door behind him.

From inside he heard Corey cuss and turn the television up so that the infomercial was blaring.

"Cuts through anything," the salesman said. "With this baby, you'll never have to fret over pork again."

He begged to differ.

BRIGGS HELD THE bottle of cough medicine up and spun it. The faint light trickling through the blinds made the red liquid dazzle. It looked almost beautiful, mesmerizing. And it was his last sip. He promised himself, no matter how many signs of withdrawal or side effects, he was going to end it. His mother could go to hell.

"Don't talk like that," she said, shaking her head. "I didn't raise my son to be a bastard."

He laughed, his eyes still on the bottle, passively reading the warning label now, though it no longer applied to him. That was aimed at those who'd overdosed but he was well past that point. He'd transcended simple poisoning. "You raised me to think I was dying. I used to be afraid of stepping outside because I thought I'd catch AIDS. You believe that? I thought it was that simple. Cancer? I thought it was crawling all over my skin. Hell, I was convinced malaria was caused by ear infections. Face it. You fucked me up pretty bad."

She started to cry and he waved her off. He'd given her the ultimate sacrifice by shoving that pillow over her hollow face that day in the nursing home, his final visit so many years ago. She'd wanted him to be sick so she could care for him, so she could be the hero. In the end *he'd* been the hero.

There was a rustling from the bed. The girl was waking up. She mumbled something and tried to open her eyes, one of which had a generous egg-shaped bruise that wasn't yet done swelling. "Glad to see you're awake."

She groaned. "I was hoping I'd dreamed the whole thing."

"Dreams don't always come true."

She tried to move her arms and noticed the handcuffs securing both her wrists. He'd locked them a bit too tightly. They would leave a mark and he wished he felt worse about it.

She brought a hand to her eye and massaged it, wincing through her teeth. "Was that necessary?"

"I said I was sorry. You didn't leave me much of a choice."

She peered around the room, her face wrinkling in disgust. He couldn't blame her. The place was a biohazard. There were close to fifty empty bottles of cough syrup scattered along the perimeter. The trash was overflowing. Dirty clothes and towels lined the carpet, which had a few more stains than when he'd first arrived.

"Where the hell are we?"

"A pirate-themed hotel. It looks like something out of a bad postcard. Cheap rates, though. And HBO is free."

"Tell me you're not really going to bring me home."

"I already had a chat with your mother while you were out. Told her we'd be on our way in a bit. In fact, I was just going to check out before you woke up."

"Really? Looks to me like you were robo-tripping and talking to your imaginary friend again." She nodded at the bottle in his hands.

He held it up. "This? Just a bad habit. Everyone's got one. Like running away from home and changing your identity."

She rolled her eyes, sat up, head bobbing from dizziness. "I didn't run away. I'm twenty years old. That means I'm not a minor and I can leave home as I please."

"The way I heard it, you left in the middle of the night without so much as a note. Your mother thought you were dead or worse. The cops wouldn't listen, said she was just overreacting. So she called me and offered a generous amount of money."

"She worries too much. Whatever she offered, I'll double it."

"That so? With the fortune you made at the coffee shop? I'm guessing you don't have much of a nest egg if your father is Clive Sherman."

Her eyes widened. "She told you?"

He nodded. "I figured it out before our conversation, though. That's kind of my thing. Look, I get the guy's an asshole. My dad walked out on me when I was two." He studied his mother for a moment. She was pacing back and forth, mumbling something, tears in her lifeless eyes. He turned back to the girl. "But you can't go killing the guy."

"That's where you're wrong." She gritted her teeth

and flared her nostrils. It could have been the syrup already starting to wear off but the look put him on edge. She was tough. He'd give her that much. "Just tell my mom I'm okay and let me go."

"We both know how that'll turn out. The second I undo those cuffs you'll kick me in the balls again—which still hurt by the way—and you'll go do something you'll regret."

She shook her head. "You don't understand. He's not just an asshole. He's hurting people. We went to where he's been staying last night and found a girl covered in blood. There will be more where that came from."

"Then call the cops if you're so concerned."

"Already tried that."

"Wish I could help but I'm tired as hell and I'd like to go home now. Let's make the best of this road trip and try to get along, shall we?"

She said nothing else, finally looking down and giving up. It wasn't a good look on her. He almost felt bad.

It was time to pack up and check out but there was one thing left to do first.

His mother, still pacing back and forth, seemed even crazier in death. She'd prevented him from having a normal life, normal friends, a wife—all of it. He'd killed her once, out of mercy albeit. He could do it again.

"Mom, can I talk to you for a minute?" He gestured toward the girl and then the bathroom. "In private."

His mother sighed. "Fine but you really need to open some windows. This place is filthy and crawling with germs."

"Can you lay off the loony stuff?" Maura said.

"Who is your invisible friend, anyway? Do you really think you're talking to Mommy Dearest right now?"

He ignored her and followed his mother into the bathroom. He turned on the faucet and the shower to block out their voices.

"Glad to see you're finally getting cleaned up," his mother said. "We should have bought you some real soap at the store. You can't trust these bars they carry in seedy places like this. Who knows what's living in them."

He wound back and hit her in the face, expecting his hand to flow through her like mist but surprised when his clenched fist made a connection. Ghost blood spouted from her mouth. Her dentures flew from her lips and clattered to the floor, vanishing, there for a millisecond and gone the next. She begged him to stop but he told her it was too late for that. He told her he hated her, hated what he'd become because of what *she'd* become. Even in her panic she still spouted lies about how sick he was. All he needed, she said, was his mother's love. But that's where she was wrong.

He squeezed her frail neck. She held her diabetic nubs, once ancient liver-spotted hands that had grown deformed by arthritis, against his fingers, tried to push him away but she was much too weak.

"I want you to repeat after me," he said through clenched teeth. "Can you do that?"

She choked out something that could have been "yes."

He nodded. "That's good. I want you to say you're the one that's sick."

Nothing came out of her mouth except for blood and gurgles.

"That's good enough for me." He smiled, laughed, and snapped his dead mother's neck. She melted into air, his hands colliding with each other in the sudden absence. He caught his breath, looked at himself in the mirror, expecting to see blood, but there was only sweat.

The remaining drop of syrup was on the sink, the bottle only inches away, but he felt better all of a sudden. He picked the bottle up, examined it one last time, and tossed it with the others in the trashcan.

"Let's get the hell out of this shitty town," he said to his reflection as he straightened his shirt and pants.

He opened the door.

And fell to the floor as the girl bashed his face with a lamp.

***

Izzy showered three more times. She couldn't shake the feeling that blood was lurking in her pores somewhere, small enough to avoid her eyes but still there on some molecular level. She fingered her scalp, expecting to find bits of flesh that had gone undetected despite the half dozen times she'd rinsed and repeated.

Fresh blood, as it turned out, was salty and not entirely unpleasant. It almost resembled the ocean if you could close your eyes and block your ears and forget about the carnage surrounding you. But Izzy could not do such a thing and some part of her knew she'd never get past last night.

She'd seen two innocent girls lose their lives. It hadn't been quick. They'd bled out slowly, twitching as their deaths approached. What were their names? Did they have families, jobs, boyfriends?

Would their parents ever know what happened? She almost didn't believe it herself but if she thought hard enough she could hear squeals and lapping tongues like they were in the next room.

She got up from her spot on the sofa, skin still moist from her fourth shower, and shivered. Didn't breathe until every light was turned on.

She paced the apartment, waiting for Liam. Hadn't he said he'd be quick? It was nearly seven now. She'd waited patiently in a stranger's home for the better part of twelve hours.

And you'll be waiting longer because he's not coming back. He's dead. Clive and his pigs or creatures or whatever they are got to him. He went after Maura. Of course he did. He's head-over-heels, thinks she's a dreadlocked goddess.

For the first time in a long time she hated being alone, needed to talk to someone—anyone.

A landline hung in the kitchen. Odd someone so young had one in the first place but she didn't question it too much. It called to her, begged her to dial a familiar number she'd been avoiding for weeks.

The last time she'd checked in with her parents, she'd told them she was okay, speaking over her father's crying pleads for her to come home. Her father, one of the biggest and toughest men she'd ever known, actually crying like a little boy.

See the pain you caused them and for what? You were bored of suburbia so you went out on your own, played some guitar, slept in the woods, and got abducted in the process.

Her pride could go to hell after the last three days. It would be good to hear her parents' voices, no matter how sad or angry they might sound.

As she stepped into the kitchen the doorknob jiggled but the door remained closed. She didn't hear the sound of a key being slid into the lock. Instead there was a pounding and scraping, someone—or something for that matter—that wanted to gain entrance.

She obtained x-ray vision then, if only for a moment. Clive stood on the other side of that door. He'd had one of his henchmen, perhaps the larger of pig things, follow them to Liam's place and confirm their location. He was feet away, camera already rolling. She told herself she didn't hear snorting, didn't detect slimy tongues licking slimy lips.

She looked around for another exit but realized there weren't any. Suddenly she was back in that room in Scary Harry's mansion. Her hands were zip-tied again and she was going to birth a fourth creature.

"Liam?" a voice said. "Liam, if you're in there, open up. I mean it."

Izzy's heart fluttered several times. All the work of showering had been overturned by beads of cold sweat. It wasn't the pig thing after all. It was Maura.

Izzy opened the door.

Maura stood in the hall, eyes wide. "Izzy? You look much better. Where's Liam?"

Izzy shook her head. "I don't . . . I don't know. I think he went to look for you."

Maura punched the doorframe. "That bastard. That stupid bastard. He likes me, for whatever reason, and he went to find me."

"Like to your apartment or something?" Izzy knew the answer to her question already. The naïve part of her mind just wanted it to be different.

Maura nibbled her thumbnail. "No, he hasn't even been to my place and for good reason. Where's the one place he'd think to look for someone as crazy as I am?"

Izzy swallowed, her throat suddenly made of sandpaper. "Scary Harry's?"

"Exactly. I've got to stop him. If anything happens to him . . . if my father lays a hand on him . . . " She trailed off, spitting a chunk of her nail onto the floor. Her eyes widened and she looked at Izzy. "You were inside, right?"

Izzy closed her eyes and nodded, trying not to think of the blood that surely still lined the foyer. She knew what came next, knew she would agree to it, no matter how stupid. She'd agree because she'd done enough crying for a lifetime. Because she was strong, damn it, had almost been killed, damn it.

And she wanted revenge, damn it.

JARED BERGMAN HOCKED a generously sized loogie and cleared his throat. No one seemed to notice. They were too busy tending to screaming children and drinking from plastic cups clearly filled with booze. About half were tourists, mumbling about how cool it was to watch a movie outside like this and the other half were locals, complaining how the tourists ruined their summer and how they wished they hadn't settled down in Bass Falls because the place was going to hell.

You're right about that, Jared thought as the tide rolled in.

He'd worked the projector for the outdoor films each summer for the last thirty years. Every Saturday night, from May to September—weather permitting—he'd drag his equipment out to the lot behind Main Street and show whatever film the Mayor told him to.

Usually it was family friendly, something with a cheesy moral message for kids, but other times it was a comedy with jokes that flew over the children's heads. On the rarest of occasions, they showed some of the old Universal monster flicks. He'd rolled through *Dracula, Frankenstein, The Mummy*, and even some lesser known gems like the *Black Cat* and *White Zombie*. But more often than not they showed crap.

You ought to really fuck with them tonight. Go grab your copy of Faces of Death *and spin that bad boy. See how long it takes for the field to clear out.*

It would be easy on account of everything being digital these days. He could pop in a DVD and wreak havoc on the crowd. The technology was demeaning. It took skill to run a film projector. He remembered kids and parents alike watching him spool the film into the reel as if he were a magician. Now he got paid to sit back and press a button. And chew some Skoal when no one was looking.

He stretched and cracked his back, checking the time. It was still light out, sunset not due for another half hour at least. He wished he could get on with it. He'd rather be on his couch with a tub of ice cream and an old cult movie.

The water was calming enough, though. As were the gulls. Most people didn't notice them or thought them to be pests but Jared felt there was something beautiful about them. When you heard gulls, you were close to the ocean, and many people in this country never saw such a thing. He should feel lucky living in a place like this even if it was becoming one big tourist trap.

Something moved just above him. For a moment he thought one of those beautiful gulls had taken a seat atop the streetlamp, probably getting ready to shit on his head. He risked a glance above, wincing and preparing for a white plop to land on his nose. The closest birds were to the left, two lamps away. There was nothing there aside from the light itself.

But that wasn't exactly true, he realized, as he heard the noise for a second time. It wasn't lifelike in its tone but mechanical, like gears turning. There was something else up there, moving slightly toward the crowd.

What the hell is that? He reached for his glasses.

The world became clearer and he saw the rusted pole and light bulb in full detail and noticed the camera perched at the very top of the structure. It was small and sophisticated, a security feature you would've seen at a bank but not a municipal lot that sometimes served as tourist parking.

He scratched his beard and tried to remember seeing it before. Surely it had been there all along and had escaped his notice.

He called bullshit. Thirty years of sitting in this lot had made him know the area better than his own bathroom. He would've seen that camera before. It hadn't been there last week. He was sure of it.

The camera buzzed to the left and moved upward as if scanning the crowd. It reminded him of a sentient being from some distant planet, a silly prop from an of the old science fiction film. Except there was nothing silly about it this evening. It made his stomach lurch and his forehead grow moist with sweat. He wiped the perspiration away with the back of his hand and noticed there were two other cameras, one on each streetlamp to his left and right. They spun on their own accord, their movements like snakes slithering through tall grass.

He turned around and saw an identical device on every streetlamp, even those in the distance on the street. It didn't stop there. There was one on top of the Tourist Trap Gift Shop, one on the public bathroom facility, and even one sitting atop the stop sign on the corner, where Main met Pleasant.

Jared had dropped acid a half dozen times in his youth. He'd heard rumors that you could have flashbacks if you cracked your neck the wrong way. The chemicals supposedly took route in your spinal fluid, waiting for the right day to pull you back into whatever nightmare you experienced. But this was no trip, no matter how badly he wished it to be. He was lucid and aware and scared out of his mind.

Something is wrong here. Those cameras weren't there last week and now there are as many as there are gulls. Those lenses feed to a screen somewhere and that means someone watches that screen. Could be watching this very moment.

His skin buzzed with electricity. The sun was getting farther away, light fading into dark. He didn't want those things to be hidden by the shadows. Didn't like the idea of those eyes watching everyone during nightfall.

He scanned the crowd for a police officer. There were usually three or four on hand. The crowd from the bars sometimes wandered down to the lot and things could get a bit rowdy.

But there wasn't a single cop to be seen, another first in the thirty years Jared had been showing movies in Bass Falls. He told himself he was panicking for no reason, that every cop had been called away for something.

He heard metal gently sliding against metal just above his head.

It's nothing. Don't look. You will not move your eyes in that direction.

He looked anyway.

The camera, like a robotic eye, was pointing directly toward him.

***

Liam fished the twenty-dollar bill from his pocket and handed it to the cab driver, told the man to keep the change. His wallet was empty now. The last bit of money to his name was the crumpled check in his back pocket. He was broke —even more broke than usual—and he would've been stressed under normal circumstances. But as the cab sped off, kicking up a cloud of dirt and dust, he knew that these were not normal circumstances.

The road to Scary Harry's mansion lay ahead, inviting him like an arthritic finger.

Not for the first time, he cursed himself.

You're an idiot, a fool, a loser. Corey was right about you. So was Heather. You came back to this place for a girl you barely know, a girl that's been lying to you. You've officially lost your mind.

Maybe so, he thought. But he couldn't let that bastard hurt anyone else, especially Maura. When you got down to it, who cared if she'd lied? Those moments spent in bed last night had been some of the best in the last year. That had not been a lie no matter what her real name was or why she'd come to Bass Falls.

He thought again of the scar beneath her tattoo, her story of Clive burning her—and that he could be hurting her again this very moment. Pigfoot or no Pigfoot, Liam wasn't going to sit back and do nothing.

He'd stopped by Walgreens then the sports store. Bought a flashlight at the former and a baseball bat at the latter, the clerk eyeing him oddly. It was the first time Liam had ever stepped foot inside the store in all his years living in his hometown. His scrawny frame and horror movie shirt didn't exactly scream athleticism.

He carried the bat now, heavy like lead in his hands, and shined the light forward. As a kid, he and Corey had walked this road plenty of times, daring to see who would go the farthest. They'd heard the rumors about Scary Harry, how he liked to capture children and make them into stews and soups. Corey had always won, taking a few steps further each time. But they'd never made it all the way and the truth was Scary Harry was mentally ill, not some monster.

Though he was likely dead now, replaced by an actual monster.

Liam tried to slow his pulse and kept walking, peering every so often into the grass and trees to his left and right. Countless shadows, each seeming to move on their own accord. He swore he heard movement with each step, though the light showed nothing but darkness. Gooseflesh warned him that he wasn't alone. There were things just beyond his line of sight. Things ready to pounce the moment he let his guard down.

Eventually the path ended at the clearing. His heart skipped several beats and he shut off the light. Pure darkness ahead. Not a single light shown through any of the windows.

That meant they were gone. They'd taken Maura, perhaps tortured and killed her on film, and escaped with their equipment. The film was wrapped.

The lot was empty, no vans or cameras of any kind. He searched the perimeter of the house, wincing each time his foot stepped on a twig or branch. The exterior was empty and somehow that seemed worse than the alternative.

The front porch, ancient and splintered, creaked as he climbed the steps. He thought about turning around but if anyone were still inside they'd surely heard him by now.

If only Corey were here to see this. Liam had won the bet after all these years. Who was the coward now? Except their friendship was likely over and no one was here to see him claim his victory.

Some victory, he thought as he reached for the doorknob, held on for an eternity, and turned it. Pushed it open, held back drops of urine that begged to stain his jeans, and stepped into the thickest shadows he'd ever seen.

He didn't want to turn on the light, couldn't imagine what he'd see. But he also didn't want the darkness, or whatever could've been standing just to his right or left, to have the upper hand. Shaking badly, he flipped the switch with his thumb and shined the beam forward.

And almost collapsed when he saw the mess on the floor.

Blood and bones and hair and chunks of things like skin and organs. It wasn't hard to imagine what had done this. His stomach rumbled, acid flowing up his esophagus, gaining entry to this mouth, and spewing onto the floor. The scent of vomit mixed with that of death. He dry-heaved several times before he could move.

He tried not to look at the mess for too long

because his mind began to reconstruct the parts, forming them into Maura.

As he stepped closer, covering his nose and mouth with the crook of his arm, he saw there were three separate skulls, the flesh already starting to decompose. It wasn't fresh enough to be her but that thought didn't calm his nerves.

He spun the light in every direction, expecting to see Clive or his crew or worse. Every room on the first floor was in disarray, trash and moldy food lining every surface but there was no sign of anyone, no equipment of any kind. He could've almost believed squatters had been living out here instead of a film crew.

He walked upstairs, the steps creaking louder than the porch. The hall to the right was just as bare. Something that had once been a sandwich lay on a cot. The bread had turned blue and the meat between looked like jerky now. Flies buzzed along the walls, swarming toward him. He waved them away.

Every room seemed empty aside from trash and bugs and a dirty mattress in the last one on the left. He looked through a window into the backyard in one of the bedrooms and saw a small structure that could've been a shed or garage. Probably nothing but it was preferable to searching the basement. He'd leave that for last, hoping he wouldn't need to search it at all.

The windows of the shed had been painted black. The shingles and wood were rotting. A spider the size of a gerbil had built a nest above the door. It feasted on something that still struggled.

Liam choked back a scream and opened the door.

A cot, a bookshelf, and a desk but no sign of life.

He was about to turn back around when something caught his eye on the desk: a pile of papers with notes scribbled along the borders.

At first glance it was a script but the more he read, the more he realized it wasn't structured enough. Mostly scribbles and ramblings. He recognized the penmanship immediately. The letters matched the signature on his check. He imagined Clive going into some trance, praying to an evil deity and receiving these words in return. The sentences were mostly incomplete. Some ended halfway through and others went on for paragraphs at a time.

He shined the light on a chunk of text at random.

The Pigfoot rapes the girls? No, too obvious. I've never done rape and why start now? Need something more creative. Maybe Tara can help.

He flipped the page and read another excerpt.

Shitty video store is perfect for hideout just before the final act. That fat fuck is dumber than I thought. Need to take care of him. Maybe use him. Would make a great death scene. Lots of blood and guts in that one.

Liam shook, almost dropped the bat. He hadn't heard from Scotty since he'd been laid off. He would call his ex-boss the moment all this madness was over. Assuming, of course, the madness would end.

He read on.

Tara showed me the final scene. Took my breath away. Gave me major wood. We fucked for two hours straight. She was cold as usual and she didn't seem to enjoy it. Didn't bother me much. Have to admit, though. Her eyes do give me the creeps. So black. So hypnotizing. Have to trust her. She says after the movie wraps our agreement is over. I'm repaying her in blood. Same thing she's said since the day in the woods. Will follow through. I owe her. Saved my life after all. Plus it's fun killing people for real for a change. Saves on the special effects budget.

Only one page left. The text tapered off suddenly. The letters sloppier, manic.

Almost time now. CJ and the boys are packing. Can't wait. Will be so much fun. Better than anything I've ever done. Pigfoot and his babies are going to shine. Tara says this is it, the final scene, the final payment. Cameras are installed. High-tech. Not sure how she managed but stopped questioning. Not human anyway. Will hide in the shitty video store until it's time. Ass Falls (ha!) showing some stupid movie downtown. Plenty of people to off. Take an hour, maybe two if we have Piggy chase them around town. Could break into a few more houses for some B roll. Either way it ends tonight. Maybe bring a couple of those cameras back and add a scene with Maura and Lisa. Bitches. Can't stand 'em. They don't respect me. They'd look good screaming for the camera. Revenge for the short end of the divorce. Will ask Tara is she can help. Hear footsteps outside. She's coming. Want to have some fun first. Horny as hell. Death gets juices flowing. Then need to head out. Almost time.

Liam read it twice more. It was hard to make sense of but one thing was clear. That bastard was out of his mind and he planned on killing a lot of people tonight.

And he hadn't gotten to Maura yet. There was still time.

He ripped the papers to shreds, tossed them like

confetti all over the dirty shack. Turned the light off and gripped the bat tightly.

He was just about to leave when he heard the car pull into the driveway.

"**M**R. BERGMAN?"

Jared barely noticed the voice. It spoke from somewhere far away, across the ocean perhaps. A radio signal, weak and distant, inconsequential. Nothing mattered aside from the cameras. They were moving quicker now, back and forth, back and forth, as if agitated.

They're getting ready, he thought. But when he asked himself *for what?* he had no answer. Perhaps that was for the best. Perhaps he ought to pack up and head home. Better still, he could get in his car and hit the highway. It was only ten minutes from Main Street. He could be on the road with Bass Falls in the rearview in less than a half hour.

"Mr. Bergman?"

Jared shook his head, looked away from the closest camera. His neck was stiff and painful from the sudden movement. He wasn't sure how long he'd been staring but he noticed the sun was just about gone, the sky three times darker than when he'd last checked. The crowd fidgeted in their seats, complaining to one another that the movie hadn't started yet.

He turned toward the voice and saw Brad Summers, the mayor of Bass Falls. Twice as tall as Jared and a third as wide, with a goatee and deeply set wrinkles that reminded Jared of Abraham Lincoln. He placed a hand on Jared's shoulder. "Mr. Bergman, are you okay?" He looked at the crowd and lowered his voice. "Because you look like shit."

Jared rubbed his eyes. "Yes, I'm fine. I mean—no, I'm not. Nothing's fine. Listen, we need to cancel tonight's movie."

"How do you mean?" Brad cocked his head and put on a fake smile as a mother and her two daughters walked by. The man was made for politics, could lay on the charm as thick as peanut butter.

"I mean we need to cancel it and tell everyone to get out of here. And fast."

"I'm not sure I follow. Is your equipment okay? We have another projector at my office if you need one."

"No, it's not the equipment." He heard the mechanical buzzing sound above, familiar by now. "Not *my* equipment at least." He pointed to the camera, its lens still watching like a displaced eye in the sky. "What do you see?"

Brad followed Jared's line of sight. "The streetlight? I know it's been flickering lately. Hell, half of them aren't working all that good. Someone brought it up at our last town hall meeting."

"Above the light, Brad."

Brad's eyes narrowed. "Is that a camera?"

"Exactly, and I'm sure it wasn't there before. And look over there and there." He pointed at the others. "Did you know anything about these?"

"Can't say I did. It's probably nothing, though. Tell you what, you start that movie for me and get these folks to stop whining and I'll look into it first thing in the morning. How's that?"

Jared shook his head. "No. I told you already. Something isn't right. You're the mayor for God's sake. Wouldn't you have heard about something like this?"

"Look, Jared, it's odd. I'll give you that much. But things slip by me all the time. I'm not the president. Not everything in town needs my permission. You'd be surprised how much flies under my radar. They're just cameras."

Just cameras? Jared begged to differ. He'd never been one to get spooked but these things had his heart thumping. He knew a hunch when he felt it and his inner voice was practically begging him to run.

"Start the movie already!" some kid in the crowd said, laughing with his buddies.

"Yeah," someone else near the front said. "We don't got all night."

Brad threw another fake smile and nodded. "Just a minute. We're having some . . . technical issues but everything is about sorted out." He turned back toward Jared. "Isn't that right, Mr. Bergman?"

Jared didn't need to see the camera to know it was focused on him. It was the same feeling you got when you know for certain someone was watching, the jolt that travelled up your spine when you walked home late at night and knew for sure something was hiding in the nearest alleyway, biding its time.

Just cameras, my ass.

"No." Jared shook his head. "Not tonight." He grabbed the projector and began to pack up.

"What the hell are you doing? It's too late to shut that off."

"Where are the cops, Brad?"

"What?"

"Look around. Where are the cops? I haven't seen one the entire evening, have you? Don't you think that's a bit strange? And don't feed me any more bullshit. I find it hard to believe they're all off responding to a cat in a tree."

Brad's nostrils flared, his face turning red. It seemed wrong somehow, like Honest Abe himself had lost his temper. "That's enough of this shit." He pushed Jared aside, reached for the projector, and pressed play.

Too late, Jared thought out of nowhere, not knowing exactly what it meant.

"See?" Brad said. "Was that so difficult?"

The crowd cheered for a moment, laughing and yelling, but their chatter died quickly when the image played across the screen. Like Jared, they'd been expecting the normal fare, some family movie about a dog that learns to play tennis or a hamster that flies to Mars but there was nothing of the sort.

Jared had seen enough horror movies in his day, knew exactly what the pig-like creature was.

Instead of puppies and kittens and cartoons, there was a clip of the Pigfoot, Clive Sherman's grindhouse mascot. It roared as it broke down a door and entered what looked like a bedroom. A man screamed, pushing the beast away and trying to find an exit, though there was only a closet, an adjacent bathroom, and a lone window, bright light streaming in through the open curtains. The scene wasn't from any of the Bone Saw films Jared had watched and he was pretty sure he'd seen them all. It looked more realistic, a snuff film with high production value.

The man on the screen backed away until his ass was against the far wall. The camera followed the Pigfoot as it kicked the man to the ground and dug in.

The crowd screamed in unison with the man as he was torn to a pulp.

✳✳✳

CJ laughed, pointing to the screen. "She did it. I don't know how but she did it. Take a look at this, boss."

They'd set up two monitors in the video store, each of them fed by the security cameras his crew had been installing each night since they'd landed in Bass Falls. Clive smiled as he watched the black and white image of the crowd. They screamed and gagged. Mothers covered their toddlers' eyes. Fathers shushed their kids and told them to turn away.

It was one of the first scenes they'd filmed in town, when they'd broken into a man's house. Robert Jenkins if Clive remembered correctly. Or maybe it was Jerry Roberts. It didn't matter. What mattered was the guy was long dead, the scene looked beautiful, and Tara had managed to feed raw footage into the projector. Technologically speaking, it was impossible. Then again, so was just about everything else about this shoot.

But Tara, sweet and beautiful and demonic Tara— she made anything and everything possible. There were no limits to her power. Not for the first time he thanked the stars he'd fallen that day. The broken ankle had been a blessing.

She watched the screens alongside the rest of the crew. Something that faintly resembled a smile crossed her face and disappeared just as quickly. It was the most human-looking gesture he'd ever seen on her. Her black eyes seemed three shades darker.

From the backroom came the sounds of snorting and chewing. They'd nabbed a jogger on their way inside the store. She had stopped to catch her breath and had been pulled inside the doorway while tying her shoe. What was left of her was presently being devoured by Piggy and his newborns. They were growing up so fast, nearly four times the size they'd been last night.

"Boss?"

Clive rubbed his eyes. "Huh?"

CJ pointed at the screen again. "I said we ought to get going. We don't want everyone running away before the fun starts." On the screens the man working the projector, the one who had been eyeing the cameras for almost a half hour, fumbled with the machinery, trying in vain to stop the film. Some lanky guy with a beard looked over his shoulder and shouted.

Should've run away when you first saw our cameras. You might have gotten out alive.

Clive squeezed Tara's hands. "What do you say? Shall we?"

He thought of the deal he'd made with her and all of the wonderful scenes they'd filmed thus far. He thought of all the time spent away from his nagging ex-wife and bitchy daughter. He thought about the film he was making, his best by a long shot. It may not have been a masterpiece but it was something else entirely. Something that defied all categories. Something new.

Tara nodded, hair swaying like shadows dancing across walls. "Yes. It's time."

Clive smiled, his hands still clasped in hers, as if they were saying their vows, sealing their love for all eternity. In a way, he thought, they were. "You heard her, boys. Let's pack it up and make our day."

CJ clapped his hands and started gathering the crew. He knocked on the back door. "Come on, little piggies. It's dinner time."

The door swung open.

Liam was as good as dead.

Lights streamed underneath the door, an engine idling and two voices speaking just outside the shed. He was cramped beneath the desk, sweating and hyperventilating. His grip on the bat was too tight, fingers tingling with pins and needles. His knees and ass had grown numb. How long had he been hiding? Ten minutes? A half hour?

All he knew for sure was that Clive and his monsters had come back for him. They'd been watching all day, had followed him back to their headquarters, had given him just enough time to dig around and come up with some answers—though each one led to twice as many questions—and now they were about to film his death scene.

Perhaps they'd just have the Pigfoot crush his skull. Knowing Clive, though, and how much of a bastard he was, Liam suspected the scene would be drawn out.

Footsteps sounded just outside the door. He risked a glance and saw two sets of feet underneath the warped wood. He imagined the lights behind the figures weren't just headlights but *spotlights*, his final scene professionally lit.

How about that? You never finished your script or film school but you got a part in your favorite director's newest film. Albeit you won't be there for the premiere.

The footsteps drew closer. Something rattled to his right, the undeniable sound of the doorknob turning. The latch unlocked and the door creaked open.

A shadow appeared on the floor in front of him. He stretched his fingers, feeling the blood flowing momentarily, and tightened his grip on the bat once again. No backing down. He wouldn't make it easy for them.

He rolled forward, jumped to his feet, and wound back.

The figure was too quick. It backed away, missing the blow by a long shot. Then they were upon him and he prepared for sharp teeth to dig into his flesh. He flailed, tried to push them away, nearly fell down. When the pain didn't arrive he opened his eyes.

It was not the Pigfoot that held its arms around his shoulders, hugging him, rubbing the back of his neck so that his pulse could at least consider slowing down. It was quite the opposite. He grabbed one of Maura's dreadlocks, fingered it like a rosary bead.

After an eternity they broke away from each other, kissed twice.

"I thought you were dead," they said in unison.

Maura laughed, though she looked scared as hell.

"I'm sorry I lied and I'm sorry I left. I didn't want you to get hurt."

He let go of the dreadlock, watched it stiffen back into place. "I'm sorry I'm stupid enough to fall for someone like you. But I'm also kind of glad."

"What the hell happened? Everything in the house is gone. It looks like they left town."

"They packed up but they haven't left yet. They're getting ready to shoot the final scene."

"How do you know that?"

He pointed at the crumpled notes or diary or whatever the hell they were. "I studied up. We need to go into town."

Someone in the doorway waved. He saw now that Izzy was just outside. "Guys?"

Liam ignored her and squeezed Maura's shoulders. "You've got to trust me. Everything Clive has filmed so far, all the people he's killed—it's nothing compared to what comes next."

She swallowed. "What comes next?"

"Guys," Izzy said again. "Will you shut up and listen?"

Above his pulse and the car's running engine, Liam heard another sound, something like waves bashing against rocks, steady but uneven, rising and falling in random patterns.

"What is that?" Maura said, eyes too wide.

He shushed her. The sound grew to a tipping point. Less like waves now and more like . . .

Screaming.

"WILL YOU SHUT that fucking thing off?" Brad said, not bothering to lower his voice and keep his political calm going. All things considered, Jared couldn't blame the man.

On the screen, the Pigfoot was still chomping on the unlucky man's face. Most films would've cut away or ended the scene by now but not Clive Sherman. He had a knack for gore that Jared had always appreciated. The parents and their children didn't share that opinion. Little girls and boys cried, wiping snotty noses as their parents cuddled them. It was their introduction to the Bogey Man, Jared thought. To their impressionable minds, the beast was just about to step out of the screen.

Who's to say they're wrong?

Jared shivered. A breeze drifted off the ocean but something told him the weather had nothing to do with the bumps along his skin. His nerves were still on high alert. He watched each camera, all of them still spinning.

"Are you even listening to me?" Brad punched the projector a half dozen times as if that would solve the problem. "You best fix this right now. You're already out of a job but if this thing doesn't shut off in thirty seconds, I'm throwing your ass in jail for the night."

"You don't think I tried to fix it? It's not me that did it. It's them."

"And who the hell is 'them?'"

Jared shivered once more and nodded to the cameras.

Brad rolled his eyes and gritted his teeth. "I've had enough of your conspiracy theories for one night. I'm driving you to the police station myself when this is over."

"They're gone," Jared said, feeling dream-like now, as if everything were out of his control. As if he himself were playing a role in his own movie. "If they were around they would've already shown up."

"Why in God's name did you think this was a good idea?" Brad said, still believing Jared was just playing a prank. He bashed the projector again. His knuckles were swollen and bloodied, matched the poor man's half-eaten face on the screen.

A couple teenagers, their eyes red and puffy from smoking too much weed, were laughing hysterically, pointing at the gore and the screaming children. They passed around a bowl and no one seemed to notice. From where Jared stood it smelled like good stuff.

Jared shoved Brad out of the way and ejected the disc from the projector, holding it up for the mayor to see. It was something called *Super Bear*, a graphic of a bear cub wearing a cape and soaring through the sky. Real cute-like. The polar opposite of what currently played.

Brad looked at the disc, turned toward the screen, then back as the disc again. The horror movie kept on rolling. "How is that possible?"

Jared rubbed his eyes. "It's not, Brad. That's what I've been trying to tell you. Something isn't right about this and I'm not sticking around to find out. You can hire a new projectionist and you can serve me a subpoena to your heart's desire. But I'm clocking out for the night." He patted the projector and walked away.

The rest of the crowd seemed to agree with him. They started packing and folding their beach chairs. All except the stoners and the obvious horror fans, drooling as the Pigfoot chomped on a convincing eyeball. Whitish fluids burst and dripped down its chin as it dug in. It snorted with pleasure.

At the edge of the lot, just along the curb, two white vans screeched to a stop, nearly hitting several pedestrians in the crosswalk. The air smelled of burnt rubber but there was something else, something rotten and sweet at the same time.

Several figures stepped out. A handful of bearded and tattooed men held equipment: a couple cameras, a boom microphone, a light. Behind them was someone that looked a lot like Clive Sherman, shouting orders to his crew and smiling uncontrollably.

Next came a naked woman, her body toned and paled but there was nothing erotic about her. If anything she was more like a corpse.

From the darkness of the second van something growled and snorted above the noises from the crowd. It sounded hungry. Sounded familiar.

Four creatures leapt from the open door. The largest of them landed on Jared and held him down while the others moved in. He struggled until his body weakened. When he finally focused on the snoutish face inches away from his own, he wasn't all that surprised. He'd known in his gut that something bad was coming but he'd chosen not to follow that hunch tonight. Which proved to be the worst—and last—decision of his life.

As the first tinges of pain filled his mind with agony, part of him, as terrified as he was, wanted to laugh at the absurdity of it all. The movie on the screen was playing out in real time, in real *life*. But that part died with the rest of them when the Pigfoot burst his skull like a cracked egg.

And slurped at his brains like a fresh yolk.

"Pull over," Liam said.

"Why the hell would we do that?" Izzy said. "What we should do is get out of here, call the cops or the state troopers or the National Guard so they can shoot those bastards on sight."

Maura gripped the steering wheel tightly, knuckles a ghostly shade of white. "We're not going anywhere but toward those screams."

Liam pointed at the small grocery store, one of many in Bass Falls that catered to tourists. They carried a small selection of necessities for those staying at the hotels. You could find Ramen noodles and Coke for triple the normal cost. But you could also find supplies for those who wanted to have bonfires on the beach. "Trust me. We'll need to hit them where it hurts the most."

Maura sighed and pulled over too quickly. Liam silently thanked the inventor of seatbelts as he tore his off and opened the door. "Leave it running," he said. "I'll be right out."

"Is there a gun store in this stupid town?" Maura had to yell over the distant screams. They were getting closer each moment.

Liam waved her away. "I've got something better. Shout if trouble comes."

He heard Maura ask what could be better than a gun but he ignored her as he stepped through the automatic doors. The distant screams grew muffled. He grabbed a basket and unfolded the metal handle, sticky with some ancient residue. The air conditioner ran at full blast, a shock against his sweat-covered skin. He rubbed his arms and shoulders as he made his way through the aisles.

A woman with bright purple glasses and badly sun-spotted skin nodded at him from behind the counter. She wore one ear bud, the other one dangling back and forth, as she filed her nails, oblivious to what was coming.

Liam found what he was looking for in the second-to-last aisle. For once in his life his encyclopedic knowledge of horror movies was coming in handy. He thought of Heather and all the times she'd rolled his eyes as he spewed forth fact after fact about special effects and behind-the-scenes trivia, all things she found useless. Now, though, that trivia was vital.

There was a thread that ran through all of the Pigfoot movies aside from the tits and teens and the underage drinking and fucking. The beast, no matter how fearless and vicious, had one weakness, one fear that the hero or heroine always seemed to exploit. It seemed too simple to be effective, yet it was the creature's downfall in all three films. Liam could only assume—could only hope—the pattern would hold true in reality.

Fire.

The Pigfoot was deathly afraid of fire. In the third film, an old hunter who had been tracking the creature, the typical harbinger of doom, told a backstory of how the Pigfoot had been made in a lab. The last in a long line of failed experiments. The scientists had barbecued the others, had themselves a luau. The Pigfoot had stood by and witnessed his unlucky peers become bacon. He'd been defeated by a flamethrower in the first film, a house fire in the second, and a grenade in the third.

He grabbed several bottles of lighter fluid, a handful of grill lighters, and a dozen cans of hairspray. The basket grew heavy, the cheap plastic threatening to snap. He brought the contents up to the front and dumped them onto the counter. The woman eyed him behind her glasses, her pupils magnified by the thick lenses. "Having yourself a barbecue tonight?"

He nodded, looking through the front windows. A man ran by the store, shouting something. "You could say that."

She punched in the prices, rang him out, placed the items into a doubled-up plastic bag. "That'll be twenty even."

He reached into his pocket and remembered he'd spent the last of his money on the cab. His fingers touched the crumpled check, the one he'd promised never to cash. He pulled it out, folded the paper, and signed on the dotted line with a pen next to the tip jar.

He slid it over and the woman eyed him oddly again. She handed him the bag of weapons and he jogged outside before she could say anything.

She followed a few moments later, shouting that she couldn't accept the payment, but he was already in the car. Maura sped off and he yelled through the window, told the woman she ought to close up for the night. There was something bad coming their way.

He wasn't sure if she heard him.

"What's in the bag?" Izzy said.

Liam pulled out the contents. "Something better than guns."

Maura raised her eyebrows, realization washing over her. "Fire. That's what always kills him in the end."

"I didn't think you'd seen your dad's movies before."

She itched at her orchid tattoo. "I've seen them all. I just wish I hadn't."

Something in the back of the car shifted. At first Liam thought they'd driven through a pothole but the street was freshly paved. The sound came again, a banging, a thumping, like fists against metal. "What the hell is that?"

Maura smirked, her eyes plastered to the road. People swarmed through the street up ahead. They were getting close. "Remember that creep that was asking about me?"

He suddenly recognized the Buick. In all the commotion, he hadn't questioned the vehicle. "You mean . . . "

"That's right. Turns out my mother hired him to come find me. She had a hunch why I'd taken off, was worried I'd do something stupid."

"Like chase after your lunatic father?"

She patted his knee. "You know me so well."

"What do you plan on doing with a guy in the trunk?"

"I'm not sure yet. But he might come in handy. You never know when you'll need bait."

Up ahead the movie screen came into view.

MAURA WASN'T ONE to reminisce. Nothing good ever came from looking too closely into the past. Hers was filled with near constant tension between her parents. The arguments and the violence hadn't come until later and in some odd way the silences that littered her early childhood were worse.

Even when things were normal, when her father had tucked her in at night, read a story of her choosing before bed, tickled and teased and played with her, there had always been something bubbling beneath the surface. It was in his eyes, some undercurrent of violence just barely held within the exterior, like a kettle slowly building to a boil.

Each time he went out to film another movie he came back a different man, a man who resembled her old father but was surely someone else, an alternate version of the man who had given her life. She knew his job was difficult, knew he worked hard to provide for his wife and daughter, but the industry had gotten the better of him. He'd gone out to Hollywood just before she'd been born. All those stupid horror movies had just been a demo reel, a way to show off what he was truly capable of. But his dreams of stardom had fizzled and he was left filming glorified snuff.

It tore him apart, drove him over the edge. He lost his sanity, beat her mother senseless both physically and emotionally. And now he was hurting strangers. She would make sure his film was wrapped before the credits rolled.

They neared the downtown lot where the weekly movie was showing. Even from here she could tell what played across the screen. She knew the Pigfoot better than anyone, except maybe Liam. It had haunted her dreams for years, an extension of her father that waited to tear her apart.

People were running in the opposite direction, banging on the hood of the car and warning Maura to turn around. She heard plenty of theories tossed about as people panicked. A riot, a bomb threat, a shooting, an act of terrorism or worse.

"Monsters," a scholarly looking man said, as if trying to convince himself he wasn't going crazy. He wore a blazer with elbow patches. His nose had been bashed and blood caked his mustache. "There are monsters down there."

"I told you," Izzy said. "I told you." She repeated it like a mantra. Maura hoped the girl wasn't reverting to the blood-soaked version of herself from last night. She needed everyone to have their wits tonight. She didn't have time to believe in monsters.

"Here." Liam passed several bottles of hairspray.

"This is our best bet." He flicked the switch on the lighter, several sparks igniting, to prove his point. "If any of those things get near us, we light them up."

"Hypothetically speaking," Maura said. "If you're right—if both of you are right—who's to say the Pigfoot is afraid of fire in real life?"

"You seemed to agree with me back there," Liam said, still emptying the bag.

"I was humoring you. Whatever's going on, it's not supernatural. Sometimes bad men are scarier than monsters."

As if on cue, like the three of them were in one of Clive's scenes, the crowd parted up ahead, revealing the lot and the rest of the screen. Revealing more screaming and pleading, more victims.

Revealing the man in the Pigfoot suit they'd seen last night.

Only it had been dark then and she'd focused on getting away. Now there were streetlamps and the fading light of evening to prove to her how realistic the costume truly was.

She slammed the brakes and watched as the man picked up an old woman like she weighed less than a pillow. She slapped and clawed at his mask to no avail. Shouldn't it have torn or ripped? Surely it was silicone or foam latex, both fragile materials. But the mask remained in place. Something like blood beaded from scratch marks along the pinkish cheek. How the hell had her father rigged *that* up?

The mask parted its mouth, revealing jagged shark-like teeth, and bit into the woman's face like corn on the cob. Her ear and part of her cheekbone came away effortlessly.

Maura's sanity threatened to flee in the wind.

It's true. All of it. Liam wasn't joking and neither was Izzy. You thought they were scared and delusional. You thought there couldn't possibly be anything worse out there than your father. You thought there was some rational explanation for all of this madness.

You thought wrong.

The Pigfoot—as real as the can of hairspray in Maura's hand—took two more bites out of the woman's face before dropping her and moving on to the next course.

Three other shapes appeared from the mass of people, slightly smaller than the fourth. They looked like miniature versions of the Pigfoot, just as Izzy had said. Piglets, she thought, and almost laughed and cried simultaneously

"I told you," Izzy said from the backseat, rocking back and forth. "I told you."

✶✶✶

"Just like that," Clive said, raising his voice over the screaming.

He stood behind CJ, ordering him to keep the camera steady. They wouldn't be using any stationary shots tonight. It was all handheld from here on. It gave a certain grittiness to the film, a certain realism.

He waved CJ closer so that the lens was inches from a bearded man who wore overalls and a flannel shirt despite the heat, a fisherman-type. Most of his face was hidden behind the overgrowth of hair but the bit that showed was picture perfect. His eyes were bloodshot and swollen as one of the piglets stomped on his head repeatedly. He'd been muttering something moments earlier, perhaps begging for mercy, but he'd since stopped speaking altogether.

Eventually his skull caved in and his eyes popped from their caverns like two snot rockets. Blood seeped from every crack and crevice, soaking the ground beneath. The piglet licked at it and snorted with joy.

Clive gave CJ the thumbs-up and they moved toward the next victim.

Tucker held the other camera, his scar like a second smiling mouth as he captured wide shots of the carnage. The crowd had cleared some but they'd grown careless in their panic. They knocked over their neighbors, trampled each other to get to the front of the line. It made for great ambience.

A kid with long unwashed hair was watching near the water, his eyes dilated much too large. He was riding high on something, paralyzed from fear and drugs.

Clive snapped his fingers at CJ and called for the Pigfoot. It charged forth, holding a rather large severed leg, and moved in on the stoned kid. The kid blocked the first few blows with his arm until it bent at an unnatural angle, bone peeking from skin.

The Pigfoot tossed the broken limb into the water and used his favorite weapon of choice. His teeth. He dug in, only stopping long enough to swallow chunks of fresh meat. Blood dribbled from its snout and Clive thought the beast had never looked so good.

It was amazing when you took it all in. He'd invented this thing over a decade ago. One drunken night, he'd started typing the first script, thinking no one would want to watch this shit. And here he was all these years later, watching his creation come to life—literally.

He walked away from what was left of the kid, stepped toward Tara. Something akin to a smile threatened to burst from her lips. She looked less pale, nearly human, as if each new on-screen kill was a sacrifice to her beauty. In a way, he supposed, they were.

"I promised you." He pushed back a stray lock of hair. "Didn't I?"

"Yes, you did. And you're following through. Just as I did."

"I never doubted you for a moment, not even when I was in that hole and bleeding to death. Part of me thought you were just a hallucination but the other part knew you were something else, something un-fucking-believable. Like I'd been waiting my whole life for you."

She nodded toward something behind him. "Now comes the true test. The final step in our agreement."

He followed her black eyes toward the edge of the lot, past the severed heads and mangled flesh that littered the ground, toward three figures walking toward Clive and his crew. They weren't running away like the others.

The one on the left was Izzy. How stupid of her to come back after escaping. The one on the right was the idiot kid who had chatted his ear off at the bar. The bruise still shown on his chin.

In the middle was the most familiar of them all, so much so that he blinked several times, thinking the face would transform, thinking he was seeing things.

Seeing his own daughter.

But it was no mirage. He knew that face, knew how much he couldn't stand his own offspring. He hadn't even wanted children, had practically begged

Lisa to get it taken care of. Maura had been a pest, a colicky little rodent that cried constantly while he tried to build up Bone Saw Studios. She'd grown to be just like her mother, a whining little bitch who wanted nothing more than to see him fail.

Even from a distance he could see her tattoo, a deformed orchid that was meant to cover up the burn, like you could change the past with a little ink. But what his daughter didn't know yet, something he planned on teaching her tonight, was that pain didn't go away. It stayed with you like a tattoo itself. Burrowed under your skull. You had to use it to your advantage, had to transfer it like a bad case of herpes.

He faced Tara once again. "You knew. You knew she would be here. You knew I'd have to make a choice."

The smile finally broke through the surface. Her wonderful face spread wide, the jagged teeth within twinkling in the last light of the evening. "Yes."

"As you wish," he said.

***

If Briggs didn't know better, he thought he'd just about lost his mind. He'd rattled and rolled around the trunk for who knew how many miles, fading in and out of consciousness, only waking long enough to puke up the little he had in his stomach. It smelled strongly of cough syrup and he'd been tempted to force it back down.

Eventually the car screeched to a stop and he heard the girl get out. All around him there were sounds that resembled screams. He kicked and punched at the trunk with all his effort, thinking he was going to die in the tomb-like compartment, until the latch finally gave and the metal lid opened a few inches.

It wasn't much but it offered him a view of his surroundings, though what he saw made him want to close it again and take his chances suffocating in the darkness.

Blood. He saw blood. Buckets of it. And other things too. Things like hearts and intestines, ears, eyes, jaws, things meant to be connected to a host, though they lay scattered along the street, separate from their owners.

What the hell had happened out there?

Something large moved past the car and grabbed onto an unlucky woman trying to make her escape. It bit into her calf with a pinkish mouth, pulling away a generous portion of leg meat. The woman collapsed and crawled away, a red puddle forming beneath her.

The thing turned toward the car. Briggs saw its face, saw the snout and beady eyes, saw the hooved hands and feet, saw his mind come undone before his eyes.

The thing from two nights ago. Pig. That's a pig, only it's not. Not entirely. It's chewing on a girl's leg. It's eating her. You've finally lost your shit.

But he couldn't blame it on robo-tripping because it had been several hours since he'd last taken his medicine. Surely it was out of his system by now. He expected to see his mother crawl out of the darkness and tell him how filthy pigs were. Hot beds for bacteria. But he was alone in the trunk, had finally gotten rid of her ghost. He was lucid, could form clear thoughts, could analyze his surroundings enough to know that what lay outside, just feet away, wasn't a figment of his imagination.

The pig thing took more bites out of the woman. She struggled for a while until it kicked her face to the curb so that her features seemed to melt away into a mangled mess. After that she stopped moving.

Briggs watched and waited, trying his best to be still. He imagined the thing looking up from its meal and locking eyes with him. He tensed, ready for death, but once the thing was finished it moved down the line toward another running figure.

This was it. His only opportunity to get out. He braced himself and pushed open the trunk.

And instantly wished he hadn't.

It was much worse than he'd thought. Blood covered the streets, forming puddles like a storm had just passed through.

He surveyed the scene and noticed a familiar figure, dreadlocks flowing in the wind, approaching a man Briggs deduced to be Clive Sherman. Could she honestly be this stupid? Whatever her father had done, it couldn't be worth dying over.

He thought of how concerned Lisa had been, ready to topple over in his office. She'd known all along that her husband was dangerous and her daughter was determined. She may have sounded surprised during their last phone conversation but she wasn't stupid.

But who cared? He ought to turn around and save his own ass. The highway was only minutes away from this bloodbath.

Don't be an idiot. She knocked your lights out, threw you in a trunk for God's sake. You owe her nothing.

She was gaining on her father, shouting what could be her last words.

Briggs didn't know how but he was certain those *things* were connected to Clive. And if that was the case, who knew what else he was capable of?

He shivered with cold sweat and made to move but his foot touched something. A bag on the ground. Inside he saw packs of tissues and a box of aspirin and, perhaps the most wonderful sight in all his life, an unopened bottle of cough syrup. Somebody in this crowd, perhaps dead now, had been fighting through a summer cold.

He lifted the bottle, removed the cap effortlessly, and drank it all in one long sip.

His shaking subsided. The sweat dried.

He walked toward Maura Black.

"**H**ELLO, SWEETIE," Clive said, his tooth twinkling in the closest streetlamp. "So glad you could make it."

Maura said nothing as she approached him.

This is suicide, Izzy thought. They were all going to die here tonight because Maura hated her father. It may have seemed more complicated but when you broke everything down into parts, that was the bottom line.

She looked at the can of hairspray and the lighter and could've laughed if she wasn't so scared. What good were they? Liam called these weapons? She didn't care how big of a movie nerd he was. This was reality, not fantasy, as crazy as it seemed. There were monsters all around her and they weren't going to be afraid of a little flame.

Maura yelled something to Clive but the sounds of people screaming blocked out her words.

When this was all over, Izzy promised herself—

knowing it would be an empty one—she would write a song about this. She'd turn it into a ballad, something catchy and calm that she could sing at a club. No more beaches and tip jars. No more slumming it.

She thought again of the phone, how she'd been about to call her parents to check in when Maura had shown up. How she'd been certain there would never again be a chance.

Something moved to her left. It was much too large and quick to be a person.

One of the pig things running toward her. It had quadrupled in size since the night before, when it had burst out of one of those poor girls. If things hadn't gone the way they had, she would have been dead on the floor with the rest of them, would have mothered a monster.

She winced at first, then she opened her eyes wide. No more being scared. No crying.

She held up the bottle, placed the lighter in front of the nozzle, knowing full well it was the last movement she'd ever make. She flicked the switch with her thumb.

Nothing happened.

She flicked it again, a small spark appearing then dying just as quickly.

The pig thing took several steps closer. It licked its lips and moaned.

Another flick of the switch.

Only sparks. Tiny, pitiful sparks.

Liam stepped in front of her and clicked the nozzle of his bottle, spraying clear mist. He brought the lighter in front of the opening and flicked the switch several times. The sparks ignited, turned to small flames that blew forth in a stream of red and orange.

The pig thing stopped, sliding forward from the momentum. It covered its blood-soaked face and mewled like an infant. Izzy almost felt bad as Liam doused the thing.

Almost but not quite.

She repositioned her own can and flicked the switch once more. This time it caught just fine, sending a second wave of fire, a miniature flamethrower, toward the creature.

It fell to the ground and convulsed, trying to wipe off the fire but failing, and she couldn't help but smile. Good. Let the thing suffer. Its skin went from pink to charcoal and she smelled something like pulled pork. Neither of them stopped until the cans ran empty and the thing had stopped moving save for the occasional twitch.

Liam tossed his can to the ground and grabbed another from his back pocket. He tore the cap off and tossed it. "Told you so," he said in between gasps for air.

Then he turned around and went after the next one.

✳✳✳

Briggs stepped over a crushed head and too many severed fingers to count. He saw the kid who he'd been watching, the kid who was also being played by Maura, lift up a can of what looked like hairspray and fry one of the creatures. It tried to run and the kid pursued, looking more insane than Briggs when he spoke to his dead mother. He was too busy fighting those things off to notice that his girlfriend was about to get herself killed.

From behind Clive stood a naked woman with what could've been the best set of tits Briggs had ever seen. They would have been distracting if one of those things hadn't come from behind her and approached Maura, its mouth hanging open and ready to feed.

He was too late. Briggs couldn't close the distance quick enough.

He stepped in something slippery. Lost his balance and slid, rolled, slid, rolled, until he landed between Maura and Clive. They were shouting, spewing insults like an argument across the kitchen table, like the world wasn't ending around them.

They each paused to look at Briggs on the ground. This was it. He'd bought himself a second, perhaps two, and he needed to use them now. The syrup spread through his veins and he felt its strength, like a warm hand willing him on. He wound his legs and kicked Clive in the groin with every ounce of effort, paying forward his own injury from the night before.

Briggs jumped up, tried to catch his balance, and grabbed Maura's arm. "Come on. We're going. Now."

She tried to pull away and he winced, thinking she'd deck him again.

"Look around," he said. "I don't know what that asshole did to you but your mother wouldn't want you to wind up as a puddle. Let it go."

She blinked as if waking from a dream, looked at the carnage surrounding them, at the charred pig thing, at the two cameras capturing everything as if it were the most normal thing in the world, just a run-of-the-mill reality show and not a blood bath. She nodded stiffly.

That was good. He'd take her back to the car and be done with it. Put this shitty town and this madness behind him. If his mother or her ghost had been around, she would've approved. He was doing the right thing.

He made to pull Maura away, glad he'd saved a life instead of taken one, when something latched onto his shoulders and pulled him back.

A stinging pain shot up his back. Warm wetness spread across his spine as he was lifted and tossed several feet toward the street. He landed on his right elbow, felt the bone splinter into a thousand pieces. He was about to turn over when something impossibly heavy landed on his back. Warm breath invaded his ears and nostrils. It smelled of shit and blood. He shivered at its snorting, but the sound was cut off quickly when his ear was torn away. Blood ran down his neck, meeting the rivers that had opened up along his back. It left his body too quickly. He felt lightheaded.

The thing came back for more, biting into his shoulder blade. He managed to force back his head, colliding with the thing's snout. It fell to the side. With the last ounce of energy in his body, Briggs flipped over.

The creature was on him again in a nanosecond. It bit into his injured arm. The flesh had grown numb. The blood that seeped from the bite seemed to belong to someone else. Briggs reached up with his remaining arm and forced his index and middle fingers into the thing's eyes. They sunk into the gooey flesh too far. It reminded him of the Three Stooges. He laughed, choked momentarily on blood and phlegm until he spat.

The beast tried to get up but collapsed, clawing at its own eyes—or lack thereof—as if they would grow back any moment.

Briggs flipped it off with his good hand, now soaked in entrails, and went limp. The world started to fade and he swore he saw an old woman break from the crowd. Surprisingly she wasn't covered with blood like just about everyone else. She looked familiar yet foreign at once. Her skin was wrinkle-free and she had the correct number of limbs. She seemed healthy, vibrant, loving. Much younger than when he'd last seen her.

His mother kneeled and patted his head while he died.

"That's my boy," she said.

"**TWO DOWN!**" Liam said, noting the twitching pig on the ground, its eyes on the pavement beside it. It lay next to the mangled body of the man who'd been talking to himself and following Liam. He'd somehow managed to get out of the trunk but he hadn't made it far.

The third spawn of Pigfoot charged for its sibling. Liam sprayed the nozzle toward the flame of the lighter. It caught quickly and he lit the creature up. It barely noticed as it tried in vain to fix the other's wound.

Liam felt a pang of sorrow but it didn't last. It passed quickly when he heard Maura scream.

He spun around and saw that Clive had his hands around her throat. Izzy pried at the fingers but one of the cameramen kicked her down, getting in closer for the shot.

Liam held up the can and ignited another stream of flames but instead of pointing it toward Clive, he aimed at the camera itself. The only thing Clive cared about more than himself was his movie—if you could call this carnage a movie. Without the film he was nothing, powerless.

He caught eyes with the naked woman behind Clive. His mind couldn't properly process her. She emanated some force, something that seemed to sizzle through the air. Somehow she scared him more than the Pigfoot, who had become too distracted with all the convulsing bodies to notice its surroundings. It was huddled on the ground, chewing too quickly, more food than it could keep up with.

Maura's face was red and purple, eyes bulging. She didn't have much time left.

Liam released the flame toward the closest camera and took great joy in watching the crewmember lose his balance and run away. The camera fell, several pieces snapping off. The spools of film within melted, the memories of this hell being erased for good.

Clive dropped Maura, looking at the ruined piece of equipment. Something passed over him, his face turning uglier than any of his monsters. He snarled, shook his head, and screamed for the Pigfoot.

The chewing sounds behind Liam ceased and he sensed something approaching.

✱✱✱

On Clive's command, the remaining cameraman kneeled, the lens inches from Liam's face. The Pigfoot pinned him to the ground effortlessly. Something dripped from its mouth and landed on Liam's lips. He tried not to think about what the fluid was.

"I've got to hand it to you, kid." Clive kicked Liam in the stomach, every ounce of air escaping his lungs.

"You've got balls. They're about to get you killed but you've got them just the same. You said you wanted to make it in this business, right? Back at that shitty bar, you told me I was your idol. And what does any self-respecting idol do? Why, they hand out autographs to their biggest fans." He nodded toward the Pigfoot. The creature seemed to understand. It ripped open Liam's *Blonde Bimbo Massacre* shirt and raked one of its claws along his chest. How ironic his death attire was day-old laundry. A laceration opened along the flesh, leaking warm blood.

"I'm afraid I don't have a pen on me." Clive pushed against the wound, Liam's blood staining his fingers. "But this should do the trick." He dipped his index finger in Liam's blood as if it were ink, and wrote two obvious letters onto Liam's forehead. Though they were out of his vision they were easy enough to identify.

F and U.

Clive laughed, slapped Liam's cheek a couple times, like he was waking him from some nightmare, only Liam's eyes were wide open, the pain forcing him into hyper-awareness, and the dream wasn't ending any time soon. "How's that look, CJ?"

The remaining cameraman smiled and nodded, still peering through the lens at Liam's impending death scene. "Looks good, boss. Nice and bloody. I think you might have your final kills here. The grand finale."

"I think you're right." The lot was mostly empty now. Whatever unlucky souls had been left behind were either dead or twitching, reaching for the stars or the crew or anyone who would listen, though their pleas went ignored. There wasn't a cop in sight. He shivered and coughed up something wet into the back of this throat.

Clive snapped his fingers. "Let's get on with it, shall we?" He slapped Liam once more. "I don't want you falling asleep on us before the final act." He nudged his head toward Maura. Liam couldn't see her. He couldn't see much aside from Clive and the Pigfoot. "She your girlfriend? You fucking my daughter? Don't look so nervous. We've all banged a few whores, right? Any port in a storm, as they say. I'll tell you what. You can choose who dies first. You can live for a bit longer and watch me kill the last of my bloodline or you can die right now. Not much of an option but I think it's fair and if there's one thing I am, it's fair." He snickered.

Liam breathed in through his nose and throat, spat saliva and blood into Clive's face. Clive wiped it away and nodded. "Good choice. The hero becomes the coward, after all." He leaned in closer so that they were nose to nose. "I want you to know that we've backed up every second of footage. Technology is a gift from the gods. And so is she." He pointed to the naked woman. "Even if you'd managed to fry both cameras and all of our gear, she would've found a way to bring them back. My movie isn't going anywhere. But you are, kid."

He smiled again, Liam's blood still dripping down his chin, that gold tooth shimmering like an extra eye, like some horrible observing appendage that was the least human thing Liam had ever seen. Clive opened his mouth, perhaps to tell the Pigfoot to finish the job, but the words died in his throat. He made a choking sound and began to twitch not unlike the bodies on the ground. Something heavy collided with his head.

Liam heard a sound like ice breaking. It reminded him of falling through a frozen pond as a child, how easy the top layer could break open, no matter how thick.

When he focused his eyes, he saw Maura standing behind Clive.

She held the bat that had been in the car, the one he'd felt so strange purchasing at the sporting store earlier.

She wound back and brought it forward again.

The tip made contact with the base of Clive's skull and the sound of shattered bone was like thunder in the night. Clive fell to his side, a steady flow of fluid leaking from what looked like a sinkhole along the back of his head.

The cameraman—CJ—made to kick Maura but Izzy stepped in, laughing, blood covering her face, and sprayed fire toward him. He dropped the camera, brushed flames off his hair. The equipment cracked on the pavement, similar to the sound of the bat hitting Clive's skull, and Izzy continued torching it until it was a pile of unidentifiable mush. Then she moved onto its operator until he too became unrecognizable. Hard to believe she'd been the same girl crying on his couch last night.

The sound guy, the light guy, and several others ran off, yelling that they didn't give a shit about this film. It wasn't worth dying over. Liam couldn't agree more.

Clive choked and heaved from his spot on the ground.

With the rest of the crew gone, two figures remained, two forms that shouldn't have been real in the first place. The Pigfoot was still on its knees, though it had since let go of Liam and was huddled over Clive, rocking back and forth. Tears—actual fully formed tears—spilled from its eyes and onto its creator's dying face. It seemed wrong, Liam thought, for such an inhuman thing to take part in such a human act.

The other figure, the naked woman, stood in place like a statue. Face contorted in disgust, disappointment. And for some reason, that scared Liam the most.

Something is going to happen.

Maura held the bat out like a sword and ordered Izzy to help Liam to his feet. Izzy managed to lift him and guided him away. "We have to hurry," she said, watching the woman and the beast closely.

"I couldn't agree more." Liam spat more blood onto the ground.

OMENTS LATER THEY were in the Buick, locking the doors and driving away from the final scene of the final Pigfoot film. Maura steered, Izzy sat shotgun, and Liam lay across the backseat. The torn remains of his *Blonde Bimbo Massacre* shirt still rested on his shoulders. He removed the fabric and pushed on his wound. The cotton absorbed much of the blood. It wasn't as deep as he'd feared but it hurt like hell and he was ready to pass out.

He would've closed his eyes then and there if it wasn't for the rumble that sounded in the distance.

"What the hell was that?" Maura said, studying the rearview mirror, her eyes wide with fear.

"I don't know," Izzy said, craning her head and looking out the window. "But I'd prefer not to find out."

"Maybe a storm's moving in." Maura drove in a zig-zag pattern, trying to avoid limbs and bodies. And blood. So much blood.

The sound came again. This time much louder and deeper, like an earthquake just beneath the surface of Bass Falls, preparing to burst through the street and swallow them whole. It vibrated in Liam's ears. He felt it in his teeth and bones. He knew, without knowing *how* he knew, exactly what the sound was. Not an earthquake or a storm. It was much worse than that.

He managed to sit up and peer through the back window.

Some part of him, no matter how horrified and defeated, was not at all surprised by what he saw in the distance: a hulking figure moving quickly in their direction, kicking aside bodies and cars like they weighed nothing at all.

Snorting with anger now that its father was gone.

The Pigfoot ran quicker than seemed possible. It reminded Liam of an eighteen-wheeler out of control. Nothing, no matter how large or heavy, would stop it from gaining. Even from here he could see the beast's eyes were red with anger. It had just witnessed the murder of its entire family. It had nothing left to lose. "Drive faster," he said, not daring to look away. "A lot faster."

"I'm trying," Maura said.

He felt the car speed up and for a moment he thought they would make it. As ludicrous as it seemed, they were going to live through this madness.

But the moment passed quickly when the Pigfoot doubled its speed and approached the car faster than they could ever hope to go.

Liam thought back to his childhood, how alienated and alone he'd felt. How Clive Sherman's movies had helped him through all the isolation, all the turmoil. In a way, Bone Saw Studios had been his mentor, keeping him out of trouble. Sure, he'd been friends with Corey but only because they were childhood chums. Their companionship had remained because of time, not choice. No one else understood him quite like Clive and his monsters.

"Turn," he said, watching the distance lessen with each moment. "Take a left or a right. Hurry." His voice was surprisingly calm for someone about to die.

"I can't," Maura said. "There are cars blocking the side streets. All of them. It's like everyone up and left." She might have been crying.

Izzy started to say something just as the Pigfoot jumped and landed on the car with a loud thud. The Buick's balance was thrown off. It swerved too quickly, threatening to flip.

"Hold on," Maura said, sounding oddly calm or perhaps defeated.

Liam didn't have time to ask her what she meant, didn't notice he wasn't wearing his seatbelt, by the time she pumped the brakes.

The car skidded for an eternity.

The Pigfoot roared as it rolled over the top of the Buick, over the hood, and onto the ground, where the front end collided with its hulking body and a parked food truck, sandwiching the beast between two solid hunks of metal.

***

Izzy had been wearing her seatbelt. She woke the quickest out of the three and for a horrible few moments, she was back in that house, with those poor girls, all of them about to become mothers. Liam and

Maura lay on the ground, had probably managed to get out of the car before losing consciousness.

The world spun. Her ears rang and her eyebrow pulsed with pain. She touched the flesh and winced, her fingers coming back moist and red. There was a matching splotch on the dashboard, where her head had collided with the plastic moments before. She was dizzy and scared but she wasn't dead. She had to keep mentally repeating it over and over like the rest of her body might not get the message and decide to shut down on her.

She reached for the seatbelt but her hand stopped at the sound of movement beneath the vehicle. The car was lifted and pushed back.

Izzy nearly screamed when she saw the Pigfoot in front of the hood. It lay at an awkward angle. Its legs were pinned under the car, its back propped against the food truck, but it didn't seem to be in that much pain. It looked angry as ever and she knew it wouldn't be long before it pulled itself from beneath the wreck and finished what it had started.

She pushed the button on the seatbelt but nothing happened. The compartment remained latched. She tried again, pulling on the fabric this time. It didn't budge.

The Pigfoot moved another few inches just fine, the car groaning in protest.

It turned its head, looked through the cracked windshield, and locked eyes with her.

★★★

Maura was kissing Liam, her arms around him, laying it on thick. She'd decided to move to Bass Falls, living together in a small apartment above the video rental store. They were at the Saturday night movie again, though this time there was no blood. The lot was filled with anxious residents, cheering as the sun went down.

A few rows to the left, though Liam tried not to look, sat Heather. He'd heard she was back indefinitely. She'd been in several features but they'd all flopped. When a deal to star in a sitcom had fallen through, she'd given up her dreams of Hollywood and moved back to her stupid hometown. Liam hadn't seen her until now. He'd been dreading the moment, thinking all those old feelings would rise to the surface again.

But he was surprised at how hidden they remained, as if they no longer existed. He couldn't stop laughing as Maura massaged the back of his head and tried to make Heather jealous.

By the way his ex-girlfriend looked, equal parts disgusted and annoyed, he thought Maura's plan was working just fine.

The crowd quieted. The movie was about to start.

He put an arm around Maura and relaxed, thinking how good he had it, thinking he'd like to sit there forever with her.

The screen lit up but instead of a movie it was a window, an actual opening in the fabric of reality, and through the glass he saw a crashed car and something that looked a lot like the Pigfoot. He heard screaming, high-pitched and never-ending, a constant loop.

He was lifted from his seat and sucked through the opening like a black hole.

And woke up. He saw the sky and thousands of stars. He saw blood on the ground, some of it from the incident at the lot, some of it his own.

He saw the Buick across the way, the front end crinkled like an accordion.

He saw the Pigfoot, kicking at warped metal, freeing itself from the car's weight.

He saw Izzy banging against the passenger window, her screams audible through the glass.

And he saw Maura on the ground a few feet to his left. She lay still, facedown.

HE PIGFOOT SLAMMED a fist against the ruined hood. It shook the car's frame, pushing it back another half inch or so.

Izzy tried the latch again but it remained stuck in place. She managed to hunch forward so that her abdomen slipped from underneath the top half of the belt. But the bottom half, the part that sealed her waist in place, would not budge.

She struggled, screamed, but the belt stayed put.

Her feet touched something hard on the floor, something she hadn't noticed until now.

An object wrapped in a paper towel, though the paper had mostly ripped and the point of the knife stood out like a beacon. Whether it belonged to Maura or the dead guy from the trunk, she wasn't sure and didn't care.

She reached for the blade but was caught off balance when the Pigfoot moved the vehicle back again. She risked a glance through the windshield and saw that the beast had freed both arms and one leg. It was getting ready to stand.

She grabbed the blade and began to slice through the belt. It barely made a mark, as if the fabric were made of bone instead. She would've been better off using a plastic butter knife. She started to cry and laugh at the same time but refused to look away from the task at hand. She sawed. And sawed. Thought of the song she'd write about all this. Though of her parents and boring yet safe suburbia.

Even when she heard the thing outside snorting and grunting and threatening to become unstuck, she didn't look, didn't blink, didn't breathe. She was going to stick the blade into its eyes. Laugh while it suffered.

After the longest few minutes of Izzy Cullen's life, the blade cut through the fabric and she was free.

As she opened the door, something else caught her eye in the backseat. The spilled contents of Liam's supplies were scattered everywhere but two items called to her.

She grabbed the lighter fluid and book of matches.

★★★

"Maura? It's okay, Maura. You're okay. Just wake up. Open those eyes for me." He brushed a few stray dreadlocks out of her face and tried not to look at the damage. Eyes swollen shut. Nose bleeding from both nostrils. Her lip piercing had been torn out, leaving behind ripped flesh he couldn't believe had been whole moments before. He'd kissed those lips. It couldn't be real. Not any of it.

But as he'd learned this last week, reality wasn't exactly set in stone. There were plenty of rules but most of them, from what he'd seen, could be broken.

He touched her cheeks. Frigid and stiff. He listened to her chest, waiting for a heartbeat. Everything was loud, he told himself. The Pigfoot was roaring and Izzy was screaming. Surely there was a pulse in there somewhere. Surely she'd wake up any moment.

Surely she wasn't dead.

But even as he told himself this, he knew it was a lie. Maura was not going to get up. He'd met and lost the love of his life in less than a week.

His hands shook as they formed fists. The world around him spun and he prepared to faint. Another scream formed in the back of his throat but it stopped dead in its tracks when he felt the hand touch his shoulder.

He spun around, pushed the hand away like a reflex, expecting a not-dead Clive or more miniature Pigfoots.

But the hand was soft on his bare shoulder. Cool, inviting. The pale woman with the black eyes. This close they became vacant caverns that went on forever.

He wanted to push her away, grab a knife and finish her off. She had been working with Clive, had helped him somehow. Perhaps she was a monster from an unreleased Bone Saw film, come to life like the others. But Liam had seen all of Clive's movies. He knew the woman was something else entirely. Something worse.

"Don't be afraid," she whispered. Her voice seemed to come from Liam's own ears instead of her mouth, as if she'd taken root in his brain. "I can help you. Would you like that, Liam?"

How did she know his name? He backed away and nearly tripped over Maura's body. Looking at her lifeless form sent fresh tears into his eyes.

"It hurts, doesn't it?" The woman's breasts swayed as she stepped closer. "Love, I mean. It isn't always a good thing. It can be just as dark as death. But lucky for you, I can help you. I can offer you a deal."

"A deal?" He sniffled.

She nodded. "I can make this pain go away. I can give you what you want most. But I will expect a payment in return. Perhaps not today, perhaps not tomorrow, but the day will come. A small price in the grand scheme of things, wouldn't you say?"

Liam wiped his eyes. "All I want is for her to wake up. For this to be over. To never feel alone again."

The voice invaded his ears again, like a soothing breeze.

"Then just say the word."

✳✳✳

Izzy crawled out of the wreck and lost her balance. She tried to get up but fell backward twice before she regained her composure.

The Pigfoot reached for her leg but she was too quick.

"You're not so scary now, are you?"

It snorted, roared. With its free leg it began to push the Buick. Izzy could see the tire was spinning. The trapped hoof would be free in seconds. She steadied her hands, unscrewed the cap on the lighter fluid, and squeezed. A stream of foul smelling liquid squirted onto the Pigfoot's face. When half the bottle was empty she moved onto the car. Soaking the hood and the interior as best she could. Her nostrils stung. Her eyes watered.

She stepped back and lit the match.

In her mind a song began to play. It hadn't yet

been written but the melody appeared clearly. She thought of a large crowd, smiling and nodding and singing along. They clapped and cheered and she didn't need them to throw coins into her dirty tip jar. Her parents were there too. She winked at them and began to sing the chorus. It sounded lovely and mellow and the onlookers had no idea the lyrics were about the darkest few days of her life.

The song grew louder in her mind as she flung the match forward and ran in the opposite direction.

She saw Liam huddled over Maura, who was waking up now, coughing and heaving but awake just the same. Izzy signaled for them to move back, to take shelter.

Her voice and the song that only she could hear were lost in the explosion. It shook the night. Chunks of metal rained down and she thought how horribly ironic it would be to die from shrapnel after everything that had happened. But the falling scraps of metal narrowly missed her as she grabbed the two others and pulled them away from the fire.

They tumbled onto the sidewalk across the street and watched as the Buick seared with flames. Within the reds and oranges lay a figure. It struggled and howled with pain, somehow worse than when it had howled in hunger. She thought for a moment the Pigfoot would crawl away, find a hiding spot and live to eat another day in a real-life sequel.

The car gave off one final burst of heat and the figure lay still.

Sirens blared in the distance. A crowd had gathered down the street, watching in horror, speculating what the hell had happened in this little fishing village.

The three of them rested on the concrete, watching the night sky and the stars, all of which seemed much brighter now.

Izzy breathed deeply and shut her eyes. She smelled something pleasant. It reminded her of childhood barbecues.

HE THREE OF them sat next to each other in a dark theater not much bigger than the apartment above his aunt's garage, though Liam had since moved into a bigger place. The room smelled of urine and popcorn, floors sticky with ancient soda residue and half-melted candy. The place was a dump but Liam couldn't stop smiling.

Six months prior he'd finished his script, after writing and rewriting it to death. Every time he was ready to rip the thing to shreds, Maura was there to talk him down, to remind him there were worse things out there than writer's block. He'd worked two jobs, saved enough to fund a short film. It wasn't a masterpiece by a long shot, screamed low-budget, obviously crafted by an amateur, but it was his. He'd finished what he'd started and that was something in and of itself. Tonight was the premier, a seedy short film festival that didn't seem the least bit respectable. You had to start somewhere.

"Are you excited?" Izzy said, sitting to his right. They'd kept in touch but it was the first time they'd met face to face in several months. She was too busy with her band. They'd been touring almost constantly, not making a fortune by any means but their name was getting out there. She had one day off during their east coast stint and she'd chosen to be here.

"More nervous than anything," he said, looking at the crowd. There were perhaps two hundred attendees, most of them filmmakers who had entered the film festival themselves. He'd only showed his piece to the hired actors, his parents (who had surprisingly liked it, admitting their son had talent after all, though it was a bit bloody for their taste), and of course Maura.

He'd invited Cory and Marcus and, against every inch of his pride, Jacqueline. No sign of them yet. Their friendship had been forced as of late. Not so far gone that it couldn't be rekindled but he wasn't sure it was *worth* rekindling.

"You'll do fine," Izzy said. "And if not, it's dark enough to make your escape quietly."

Maura patted his thigh. "She's right but I won't let you. If you make a run for it, I'll tell them to turn on the lights and we'll all throw this shitty popcorn at you. So you best stay in your seat and stop being a baby." She winked at him and he found himself traversing that familiar mental road, the one where every sign seemed to point in the same direction, reminding him of something he tried each day to forget.

I will expect a payment in return.

He swallowed, his throat suddenly dry despite several sips of flat soda.

Perhaps not today, perhaps not tomorrow . . .

"Shh." Maura took his hand into hers. "It's starting."

The lights dimmed and the projector started humming.

For a moment, he swore there was someone next to Maura, though the seat had been empty seconds before. Not Corey or Marcus sneaking in at the last minute. Not even Jacqueline. He could just make out a pale form in his periphery. He begged himself not to turn, not to look at the woman with the black eyes, but he was too weak.

He spun his head and saw that the seat was empty again, though it didn't feel that way. He hadn't felt alone—even when he *was* alone—for quite some time.

Maura squeezed his hand. "What're you looking at?"

He smiled, turning his head toward the girl with the dreadlocks who had almost gotten him killed more than once. "Nothing. Just you."

"Well, look at me later and watch your movie."

"Sounds like a plan."

The opening credits began to roll.

ACKNOWLEDGEMENTS

In addition to the immortal Max Booth III and Lori Michelle for all their help with my writing career, thanks to Emily Pineau, Ryan Beauchamp, Adam Cesare, Max Linsky, Matt Serafini, Scott Cole, Matt Hayward, Tony Tremblay, Aaron Dries, Kristopher Rufty, Mike Lombardo, Bracken MacLeod, and my parents for allowing me to watch horror movies at a criminally young age.

ABOUT THE AUTHOR

Patrick Lacey was born and raised in a haunted house. He currently spends his nights and weekends writing about things that make the general public uncomfortable. He lives in Massachusetts with his fiancee, his Pomeranian, his over-sized cat, and his muse, who is likely trying to kill him. Follow him on Twitter (@patlacey), find him on Facebook, or visit his website at https://patrickclacey.wordpress.com/

IF YOU ENJOYED *BONE SAW*, DON T PASS UP ON THESE OTHER TITLES FROM PERPETUAL MOTION MACHINE . . .

INVASION OF THE WEIRDOS
BY ANDREW HILBERT
ISBN: 978-1-943720-20-0
Page count: 242
$16.95

After getting kicked out of his anarchist art collective for defending McDonald's, Ephraim develops an idea to create a robot/vending machine with the ability to hug children. He is no roboticist, but through dumb luck manages to hook up with a genius—a like-minded individual who also happens to be the last living Neanderthal. Meanwhile, a former personal assassin for a former president is fired from the CIA for sexual misconduct with a couple of blow-up dolls. He becomes determined to return to the government's good graces by infiltrating Ephraim's anarchist art collective in the hopes that they are actually terrorists. What follows is a bizarre, psychedelic journey that could only take place in the heart of Austin, Texas.

THE GREEN KANGAROOS
BY JESSICA MCHUGH

ISBN: 978-0-9860594-6-9
Page count: 184
$12.95

Perry Samson loves drugs. He'll take what he can get, but raw atlys is his passion. Shot hard and fast into his testicles, atlys helps him forget that he lives in an abandoned Baltimore school, that his roommate exchanges lumps of flesh for drugs at the Kum Den Smokehouse, and that every day is a moldering motley of whores, cuntcutters, and disease. Unfortunately, atlys never helps Perry forget that, even though his older brother died from an atlys overdose, he will never stop being the tortured middle child.

Set in 2099, THE GREEN KANGAROOS explores the disgusting world of Perry's addiction to atlys and the Samson family's addiction to his sobriety.

THE DETAINED
BY KRISTOPHER TRIANA
ISBN: 978-1-943720-26-2
Page count: 112
$12.95

When Phoebe McBride returns to Bonneville for her twentieth high school reunion, she tells herself it's the best way to confront what has haunted her since her senior year. There was one boy who never lived to see graduation, and in a way she blames herself for this tragedy. Now a child psychologist, Phoebe is determined to face her demons by going back, but those demons may be fresher than she realizes.

When she arrives at the school there are only three of her old classmates present—a bad boy turned writer, a fallen football hero and a popular girl whose life isn't all she'd thought it would be. Bonneville isn't even set up for a party—it's set up for detention. Tables are aligned and her old P.E. teacher sits waiting. He always hosted detention back in her school days, but now he thinks he's here to accept an award for all his years of service.

Soon the guests discover gruesome keepsakes waiting on their chairs. Horror and paranoia sink their claws into the class of '96 as they are forced to revisit the worst memory from their youth, and ultimately pay for their past.

The Perpetual Motion Machine Catalog

Baby Powder and Other Terrifying Substances | John C. Foster | Story Collection

Bleed | Various Authors | Anthology

Crabtown, USA:Essays & Observations | Rafael Alvarez | Essays

Dead Men | John Foster | Novel

Destroying the Tangible Issue of Reality; or, Searching for Andy Kaufmann | T. Fox Dunham | Novel

The Detained | Kristopher Triana | Novella

Gods on the Lam | Christopher David Rosales | Novel

Gory Hole | Craig Wallwork | Story Collection (Full-Color Illustrations)

The Green Kangaroos | Jessica McHugh | Novel

Invasion of the Weirdos | Andrew Hilbert | Novel

Last Dance in Phoenix | Kurt Reichenbaugh | Novel

Like Jagged Teeth | Betty Rocksteady | Novella

Live On No Evil | Jeremiah Israel | Novel

Long Distance Drunks: a Tribute to Charles Bukowski | Various Authors | Anthology

Lost Signals | Various Authors | Anthology

Mojo Rising | Bob Pastorella | Novella

Night Roads | John Foster | Novel

Quizzleboon | John Oliver Hodges | Novel

The Perpetual Motion Club | Sue Lange | Novel

The Ritalin Orgy | Matthew Dexter | Novel

The Ruin Season | Kristopher Triana | Novel

Sirens | Kurt Reichenbaugh | Novel

So it Goes: a Tribute to Kurt Vonnegut | Various Authors | Anthology

Speculations | Joe McKinney | Story Collection

Tales from the Holy Land | Rafael Alvarez | Story Collection

The Nightly Disease | Max Booth III | Novel

The Tears of Isis | James Dorr | Story Collection

The Train Derails in Boston | Jessica McHugh | Novel

The Violators | Vincenzo Bilof | Novel

Time Eaters | Jay Wilburn | Novel

Vampire Strippers from Saturn | Vincenzo Bilof | Novel

Patreon:
www.patreon.com/pmmpublishing

Website:
www.PerpetualPublishing.com

Facebook:
www.facebook.com/PerpetualPublishing

Twitter:
@PMMPublishing

Newsletter:
www.PMMPNews.com

Email Us:
Contact@PerpetualPublishing.com

CPSIA information can be obtained
at www.ICGtesting.com
Printed in the USA
LVHW101339090422
715657LV00001B/89